GLORIOUS

a novel by
Bernice L. McFadden

Published by Akashic Books
©2010 by Bernice L. McFadden

ISBN-13: 978-1-936070-11-4
Library of Congress Control Number: 2009938474

First printing
Printed in Canada

Akashic Books
PO Box 1456
New York, NY 10009
info@akashicbooks.com
www.akashicbooks.com

. . . and the end of all of our exploring
will be to arrive where we started
and know the place for the first time.
—T.S. Eliot

For my daughter, R'yane Azsà Waterton,
who is the best part of me

A Note from the Author

While this work is built on the foundations of historical events, in many instances I have knowingly altered facts and dates to suit the purpose of the story.

PROLOGUE

If Jack Johnson had let James Jeffries beat him on July 4, 1910, which would have proven once and for all that a white man was ten times better than a Negro, then black folk wouldn't have been walking around with their backs straight and chests puffed out, smiling like Cheshire cats, upsetting good, God-fearing white folk who didn't mind seeing their Negroes happy, but didn't like seeing them proud.

If Jack Johnson had given up and allowed James Jeffries to clip him on the chin, which would have sent him hurling down to the floor where he could have pretended to be knocked out cold, then maybe Easter Bartlett's father wouldn't have twirled his wife and daughters around the house by their pinky fingers and his son John Bartlett Jr. wouldn't have felt for the first time in his life pleased and glad to be a black man. And if Jack Johnson had let the shouts of "Kill that nigger" that rang out from the crowd unravel him or the Nevada heat irritate him, maybe then he would have lost the fight and things would have remained as they were.

Things could have gone a different way if Jack Johnson hadn't gotten the notion some years earlier to cap his teeth in gold, so his smile added insult to injury when he was announced the victor of the "The Fight of the Century," and that glittering grin slapped white folk hard across their faces.

And if John Bartlett Sr. hadn't bet on Jack Johnson to win, then he wouldn't have had the extra money to buy his wife and two daughters new dresses from the most expensive dress shop in town, and the older of the two girls called Rlizbeth wouldn't have let her hair down and donned that brand-new yellow dress that made her look like an angel, so those white boys wouldn't have noticed her, wouldn't have called out to her from across the road, wouldn't have followed her and jumped her just as she reached the bend and dragged her into the brush, where they raped and beat her.

If all of that hadn't happened, then Easter wouldn't have looked up to see her sister crawling home on all fours like a dog, with a bloodstain shaped like the state of Texas on the backside of Rlizbeth's dress. Easter wouldn't have bore witness to the bite marks on Rlizbeth's breasts, and wouldn't have heard the silence that streamed out of Rlizbeth's mouth when she opened it to scream.

No sound at all.

Because after the first boy rammed his dick inside of Rlizbeth, her voice floated up into the sky never to be heard from again. And Easter wouldn't have had to accompany John Sr. down to the sheriff's office because her mother wouldn't let him go alone and wouldn't—couldn't—send John Jr. because that boy hadn't unclenched his fists or his jaw since it happened, and besides blood was swimming in his irises and he claimed to hear it thumping in his ears, so Easter went and then watched her father change from a man to boy right before her very eyes.

And if Sheriff Wiley had not forced Easter and her father to stare at the filthy soles of his boots, because it had not suited him to remove his feet from atop the wooden desk, and if Wiley had looked them straight in the eye like he would have his own kind instead of watching them from beneath the shade of the wide-brim hat he wore, and maybe if he'd believed John Sr. when he said, "I knows it was white boys cause we found tufts of blond and red hair clutched in Rlizbeth's hands," and Wiley had just gone out and found those boys and arrested them instead of suggesting that Rlizbeth had torn her *own* dress, bit her *own* breasts, and broke her *own* hymen all in order to cover up the somewhere or someone she had no place being or seeing—then maybe life for Easter would have been different.

But Wiley didn't do the right thing, and Easter looked up at her father who sat next to her with his head bowed and she heard his timid voice say, "Yes suh, I suppose you could be right, but how do you explain the hair? The red and blond hair?"

Wiley said he couldn't explain it and then dismissed them by tugging the brim of his hat down over his face and bid them a good day. If he hadn't done that and Easter hadn't seen the tears welling up in her father's eyes, she wouldn't have turned into the snarling howling thing and her father wouldn't have caught her by the waist just as she leapt across the desk intent on tearing out Wiley's throat.

If Jack Johnson hadn't been quite so dark and hadn't pumped his fists in the air like the champion he was then maybe . . .

If Rlizbeth had just put on one of the old, worn

dresses she owned and kept her hair pulled back in a tight bun, Easter probably never would have written the word HATE on a piece of paper, crumpled it into a ball, dropped it in a hole in the ground, and covered it with dirt, and her mother wouldn't have tried to go back to living as if that awful day hadn't happened and those boys weren't walking around as free as birds, and she never would have had the strain of pretending that everything was normal even though Rlizbeth had lost her voice and John Jr. had taken to staring down every white man in the town and John Sr. was intent on trying to make himself grow big again and thought that taking refuge in the arms of another woman would help him do that.

And if Zelda hadn't found the love letters pressed into the pages of her husband's Bible, letters written on fine onionskin paper that smelled of rose water, then John Jr. wouldn't have caught her crying, wouldn't have seen the letters scattered on the floor, and wouldn't have hit his father so hard that it knocked the wind out of both men. If all of that hadn't happened, then John Jr. wouldn't have had to leave the house, the town, and the state, and Easter might have gone on loving and respecting her father. But it did and Zelda's heart snapped under the strain, pain, and betrayal, and she died.

If there had not been a funeral, there would not have been a repast, so there would have been no need for Easter's father to wait patiently for the last mourner to leave the house before he changed his clothes, mounted his horse, and galloped off into the night leaving the scent of his pipe tobacco hanging in the air. And if he hadn't left, then he couldn't have returned with the wide-eyed, milky-brown woman who smelled of rose water and wasn't much older than Rlizbeth. He couldn't have brought her into their home, told Easter and Rlizbeth her name—which was Truda—and then informed them that she was his new wife and their new mother.

If Jack Johnson had just thrown the fight and Rlizbeth had maybe walked down a different road and not have been so pretty, everything would have remained the same in their small home and Easter would not have known the aching sadness of a dead mother, gone brother, and mute and ruined sister. And if there were no ache and no sadness then Easter would not have taken the gown that her mother died in, laid it across the dining room table, and arranged the china, crystal, and the silverware with the scrolled handles on top of it as if it was a special holiday and the family was expecting dinner guests. And she would not have placed bunches of flowers at the neckline, hemline, and sleeves—but she did, and when Truda walked into the dining room the next morning she forgot to breathe.

And if Truda hadn't forgotten to breathe, then maybe she wouldn't have screamed, which of course brought John Sr. into the room to see what was the matter. After that he kicked in the door to Easter's bedroom and found her sitting at the edge of the bed staring at her palms. He charged in and loomed over her like a great black hawk and hollered that he should have drowned her at birth. And if he hadn't said those hurtful words, Easter would have stayed in Waycross, Georgia, married, had children, grown old, and died.

But on that summer day in 1910, Jack Johnson did beat James Jeffries and Rlizbeth did put on that yellow dress that made her look like an angel and nothing and nobody was ever the same again.

BOOK I

FLIGHT

CHAPTER 1

Sixty-three miles of road streamed out before her like a black snake. Easter walked until an old man with a golden beard wearing a top hat pulled back the reins of his horse and invited her to hop aboard his carriage.

"Where you headed?"

"Valdosta."

The horse clumped along while the owls hooted and blinked their pumpkin-colored eyes and the darkness behind the trees rolled, writhed, and reached out to touch them.

Easter arrived in Valdosta just as dawn ruptured the night sky. She remembered the street called Cotton Way and the little stream and wooden footbridge. The footbridge was still there, but the stream had turned into a gulley, thick with mud. She remembered the house being white, but the years had streaked an unflattering gray across its once-bright, planked face.

"Who you?" the woman, who looked so much like her mother, peeked around the door and asked.

"Zelda's girl." Easter gripped tight the handle of her suitcase. Behind the house a cock heralded the new day. Thunder boomed a town away and the air began to whip.

The woman said, "Who?"

"Your sister, Zelda. You Mavis, right?" Easter's voice was hopeful.

Mavis wrapped her arms around her chest. "My sister Zelda's been dead for more than a year, so I hear."

"Yes."

Easter peered over Mavis's shoulder into the dark shadows of the house.

"Lots of women named Zelda been dead for more than a year. How you know you got the right house? I ain't never seen but one of her chirren and that was a boy."

"That would be my brother, John Jr."

Mavis dug a finger into her ear and scraped. "You do, I guess, got some of her features."

The two women eyed each other. Mavis rested her hip against the jamb of the door. She looked down at the suitcase.

"You runnin' from something?"

"Runnin' toward something."

Mavis nodded, "The law looking for you?"

Easter shook her head no.

Mavis's eyes moved to Easter's midsection. "You in trouble?"

"No, ma'am."

"Good, cause I can hardly feed the chirren I got."

Easter followed her in and tried hard not to stare at the hump on her back.

They stepped straight from the porch into the kitchen. Stove, icebox, round table with five mismatched chairs. A rope had been strung between the walls and a sheet thrown over it, hiding the window and the bed with two sleeping children. At the back of the house was one large room, beyond that the outhouse.

"What she die from?"

Easter thought for a moment and then said, "A broken heart."

Mavis made a face. "Sorry to hear 'bout that. Mens bring us womens nothing but heartache." She shook her head and sighed heavily. "You gonna have to share a bed with my eldest girls," she informed Easter as she moved to the icebox. "I s'pose you hungry?"

Mavis set the cheese on the table, walked over to the far wall, and retrieved a tin of crackers from the shelf. "I got five kids and no man, but we get by okay, better than most folks I guess. Everybody work, 'cept the babies of course, they two and four."

Easter sat down at the table and watched Mavis light the stove.

"I'll make you some tea. This all I got to offer you, wish I had more."

Easter was grateful.

"Miss Olga needs a girl," Mavis continued as she set the kettle on the stove and then pulled at the knot in the scarf she wore on her head. "She lives in town, big white house, black dog in the yard. Take a piece of meat, he'll let you in with no problem if you feed him."

Easter nodded.

"They call her the librarian on the account that she got like a million books."

Easter loved books.

The next day Easter went down to Miss Olga's house with a saved piece of bacon from her breakfast. The dog, Blackie, snarled and bared his teeth. Easter tossed the bacon over the fence and Blackie gobbled it up. His eyes went soupy and he wagged his tail and followed Easter to the back porch. A brittle, bald-headed man met her at the door. His one good eye rolled from the top of Easter's head down to the rounded toe of her shoes and then up again. "They call me Slim."

And slim he was. As straight and thin as a line. Easter told him that she was inquiring about the job and he pushed the screen door open and invited her in.

The kitchen was large and sunny. A woman stood over the sink, her hands immersed in dishwater; she looked at Easter and smiled.

"This here is Mary Turner," Slim announced in a raspy voice before scurrying from the room.

Easter said, "How you?"

Mary Turner was young and stout with rosy cheeks. "I'm blessed, thank you. How about yourself?" she said as she reached for the pot that hung from a hook high above her head.

"I'm fine." Easter pointed to Mary's full-like-the-moon belly. "When you due?"

Mary announced that she had just four months to go.

Easter's eyes glided over the brass pots and sparkling tile. Something good was bubbling on the stove and Easter's stomach churned to taste it.

The door swung open and Slim called to her, "Missus say come on in." His voice dropped to a whisper, "But make sure you keeps your feets on the floor. She don't like people stepping on the carpet, it come all the way from India."

Easter walked through the dining room and into the front parlor where bookshelves covered every inch of wall space and climbed all the way to the ceiling. Olga Fields was stretched out on a chaise lounge awash in morning sunlight the color of candle wax. In her hands she held sheet music, her thin lips moving soundlessly to the melody.

"Mornin', ma'am."

Olga's eyes remained fixed on the stanza. "Who sent you here?"

"My aunt."

"And who is your aunt?"

"Mavis Hawkins, ma'am."

"Yes, I know her. She takes in my laundry. She seems to be a decent woman."

Mrs. Olga raised her violet eyes and peered at Easter over the thin rims of her glasses. After a moment she summoned her closer with a wiggle of her index finger. Her mouth curled into a smile as she watched Easter carefully navigate the edge of the carpet.

"That's good, you know how to follow instructions. Do you know how to cook?"

"Yes, ma'am."

"You'll be helping Mary prepare the meals among other things. Slim will advise you of your duties. I pay two dollars a week and the leftovers can be divided between yourself, Mary, and Slim."

"Yes, ma'am."

Three weeks later Lawton Fields, Mrs. Olga's husband of twenty years, returned from his trip abroad. He was tall and lanky with narrow blue eyes and a bulbous nose that protruded from the center of his face like a cauliflower. He was not an attractive man by any stretch of the word. Olga was no great beauty herself, but certainly appealing enough to have snagged a better-looking man than Lawton. The truth was that the two were a perfect match. Both were liberal thinkers and curious about the world. However, Olga's phobia of great bodies of water only allowed her to experience the world through her beloved books.

Lawton had an adventurer's heart and traveled often and for great lengths of time. When Easter first laid eyes on him, he was returning from a four-month expedition to South Africa, where he had retraced the footsteps of his hero, the great missionary and explorer Stanley Livingston.

The sight of Easter drew his breath away, as she held a striking resemblance to the women of the Khoisan tribe.

When she walked into the dining room, a plate of sausage balanced in her hand, he looked up into her face and his memory swept him back to South Africa. The hairs on his arms rose just as they had when his feet first stepped onto African soil. It was a magical place, that Africa.

"What's your name?" he asked, looking deep into Easter's eyes.

"Easter, suh."

"Easter." He repeated her name as if savoring something tasty. Olga's brow arched and Lawton sunk his fork into the plump flesh of the sausage.

CHAPTER 2

Easter, Mavis, and the older children carried the scant pieces of furniture from the house and set them down in the front yard beneath the hot Georgia sun. The chintzes swarmed and the children screamed and pointed as the tiny black bugs made a beeline to their death.

Easter soaked rags in camphor oil, dropped them into cooking pots, and set them aflame, filling the house with smoke, killing the chintzes that remained hidden in the walls.

Outside the younger children played tag and hide-and-go-seek. Mavis sat in her rocking chair with her eyes closed and Easter laid herself down beneath the shade of the tupelo tree and read.

Over the past few months it had been her great pleasure to work for Mrs. Olga. The woman had recognized Easter's intelligence early on and did not miss the longing that flashed in her young employee's eyes whenever they swept across the hundreds of books that lined the shelves.

"Can you read?" she'd asked one day as Easter rubbed mineral oil into the wood moldings around the doorway.

"Yes, ma'am."

"Really? Who have you read?"

Easter rattled off an impressive list of writers and their works. Mrs. Olga was flabbergasted, she had never met a well-read Negro. "Well," she said as she removed her glasses and rubbed the strain from her eyes, "you are more than welcome to borrow any book that strikes your fancy."

Easter was delighted, and devoured four books in just as many days. She read deep into the night. She read until the flame of her candle burned down to wick.

The two women discussed, in depth, the books that Easter had read. Mrs. Olga was impressed with her insight and was happy to find that Easter's aptitude stretched beyond the frivolity of the dime-store romances most of the women in her generation swooned over. Olga started to feel that she had found a kindred spirit in the young Negro maid.

The day began to slip away and the sun swelled until it was blood-orange and then began its descent. Mavis and Easter went into the house, raised the windows, and opened the doors. They swept the dead chintzes into a black pile in the middle of the floor and then scooped them up and sprinkled them into the flames that crackled and spit in the fireplace. They moved the furniture back into the house and Mavis made a dinner of boiled yams, snap peas, and stewed chicken feet. The children were fed and put to bed. Mavis and Easter were sitting at the table enjoying a slice of pecan pie when the sound of a shotgun blast ripped through the quiet. The children bolted out of their beds, Mavis's fork clattered loudly to the floor, and Easter pressed her hand to her heart. A second shot sounded soon after the first and everyone dropped to the floor. They waited for a third shot, but none came, just the pounding of fleeing feet. They crowded under the table, trembling and clutching one another, until the flame in the oil lamp burned out and the house went as black as the deed that had been done.

The following day, clusters of people gathered along the road, on porches and out in front of the general store, and the story of what had taken place the previous night jumped from one mouth to the next. A white man named Hampton Smith had been shot dead as he sat taking his supper. The second bullet had struck his wife in the shoulder.

"That nigger done gone and lost his mind," Mavis's neighbor, a widower named Bishop Cantor, said as he eased himself down onto the porch step, removed his hat, and fitted it onto the broad cap of his knee.

Easter stood near the doorway, her hands clamped at her belly.

"Who?" Mavis asked.

Bishop dropped his eyes and mumbled something Mavis didn't quite hear.

"What you say, Bishop?" she hissed, stooping down alongside him, her youngest child straddling her hip.

Bishop drummed his fingers on the rim of his hat. "They say Sidney Johnson was the one that done it."

Mavis puckered her lips and shook her head pitifully. Her knees cracked when she rose.

Bishop saw the dark wetness on the material of her dress. "Boy needing changing," he grunted before he placed his hat back onto his head and stood. "Sidney must be miles away by now, and done left a heap of trouble behind him. White folk gonna make sure somebody pay, don't matter who, jus' as long as it's one of us niggers."

Mavis nodded her head in agreement and reached over and pulled a rotten splinter of wood from the railing.

"It's gonna be hell here," Bishop declared. "White men with shotguns coming in by the wagonload since six this morning." He pressed his palms into his lower back and stretched. "Mavis, make sure you keep your boys close to home, ya hear?"

And with that he was gone. Mavis blinked and saw the gray of his shirt disappear around the corner of the house.

The killing spree started that evening. Three innocent men were lynched over just as many nights, and on the dawn of the fourth day a woman's terrified screams echoed through the blue darkness. "Another one," Easter gasped as she tiptoed to the front door.

"A woman?" Even as Mavis uttered the words she couldn't believe it.

"Who you think they got?" Easter whispered.

Mavis stared wide-eyed.

The two women had used the kitchen table and chairs to build a barricade in front of the door and now Easter began to quickly dismantle it.

"What you doing?" Mavis's voice was filled with panic.

Easter ignored the question. "Help me move this table."

Mavis backed away. "I will not!"

Easter summoned all of her strength and pushed. The table slid across the floor and Easter pulled the front door open and stepped out onto the porch.

"Git your black ass back in here, gal, are you crazy?"

The torch-wielding mob stomped past the house and Easter hitched her gown above her ankles and started after them. Mavis didn't call to Easter again. She watched her niece sprint down the road and was sure it would be the last time she would see Easter alive and so turned her face to the heavens and asked God to make Easter's death swift and painless.

Taking shelter behind a tree, Easter stood, unnoticed, not more than three feet from a mother who had her arm wrapped casually around the shoulders of her young son.

The abducted woman shrieked out again. Easter recognized the voice and the hairs on the back of her neck stood up. The crowd parted and Easter's eyes fell on Mary Turner's terrified face.

Mary stood whimpering and shivering with her arms wrapped protectively around her swollen belly.

Someone yelled, "String the bitch up!"

Isaac, a big, brawny, red-haired man, shoved Mary hard to the ground and two men rushed forward, one bracing her flailing legs, the other pinning her arms, both taking pleasure in digging their dirty fingernails into her brown flesh. Isaac wound the coarse lynch rope once, twice, three times around her ankles, and then did the same to her wrists.

"Castor!" Isaac turned to the crowd and yelled for his son. "Castor!"

The woman who stood spitting distance from Easter bent over and whispered in her son's ear, "Go on, Castor, your daddy's calling you."

Castor dutifully trotted over to Isaac and a jubilant cheer rose up from the crowd.

"This is my boy's first lynching!" Isaac proudly announced, and he handed Castor the tight end of the rope. The boy appeared to Easter to be no more than five years old. Isaac hoisted his son up and onto his broad shoulders. "Toss it over the limb," Isaac instructed, which Castor did successfully on his first try.

Ten pairs of hands and dozens of mouths heaved and hoed and Mary's body slowly rose up . . . up . . . up . . . until she swung like a pendulum, ticking away the seconds until she would be dead.

Someone threw a stone that struck her over her eye. The next stone caught her squarely in the center of her forehead. The third one sliced her cheek, all this as Mary begged for her life and her eyes cried a waterfall of tears.

There was a splashing sound and the night air was suddenly filled with the scent of gasoline.

Again Castor was called upon. His father handed him a torch and Castor wrapped his small fingers around the stem. The flames cast a luminous light across his face. The boy was smiling. Time stopped for a moment, and when it started again Mary was ablaze. She screamed, a horrible, haunting scream that would stalk the dreams of Valdosta's residents for years. Her body jerked and twitched wildly as the flames quickly engulfed her and she was dead.

Then the vilest thing happened, the thing that turned the stomachs of even the evilest members of the group. A young man, maybe sixteen, maybe younger, fought his way to the front of the crowd; his arm was raised, shielding his face from the heat of the flames. In his other hand he clutched the wooden handle of a rusted machete. He charged toward Mary with the machete held high above his head and when he was in striking distance he brought it down in one precise stroke and the blade split Mary's belly clean open.

The infant tumbled bloody and squirming from her womb, careening downward, stopping just inches above the ground, its impact thwarted by the umbilical cord.

The air sucked away. Some women bent and spilled sick onto their feet. Others clasped their hands over the eyes of their children. The men looked away and then looked back again. The second swing of the machete severed the cord and the baby hit the ground with a soft thud and uttered a pitiful wail.

Isaac looked around and saw that shame had replaced the rage of the crowd and one by one the people turned their backs on him and started home.

Castor peered down at the crying infant, then up at his father. "Can I have it, Daddy?"

Isaac shook his head, raised his foot, and brought the heel of his boot down onto the baby's skull.

The following day Valdosta was as quiet as a crypt and Easter was packing to leave.

"They turn on you," Mavis murmured as she watched Easter throw the few pieces of clothing she owned into her suitcase. "I don't know why, but they do." She sat down on the bed and pulled her knees to her chest. In that moment Mavis looked just like Easter's mother, and Easter almost cried.

Mavis smoothed her hand absentmindedly across her hair. "You know, Mary nursed that boy when his mama was too sick to do it herself."

"Which boy? The one that cut her?"

Mavis shook her head no and leaned back on her arms. "Castor, the one that lit the flame."

Easter glanced around the space to make sure she had everything. When she looked back at Mavis she said, "You should come with me. You and the children."

Mavis stood and wrapped her arms around Easter and squeezed. "You don't even know where you're going."

"Any place gotta be better than here."

Mavis stepped away and snorted laughter. "Girl, every place the same as here, they just go by different names. Anyway, I'd rather stay here and deal with the devil I already know."

CHAPTER 3

Part vaudeville act, part circus, Slocum's Traveling Brigade crisscrossed backwoods America, entertaining Negroes barely forty years free of slavery who were uneducated hard workingmen and -women who, when told to sign on the dotted line, all had the same name: X.

They went to the jig show, clutching their nickels and pennies. The men tucked pints of moonshine safely into the back pockets of their overalls and wore their straw hats slung back on their heads, as they looked on in awe at the fire-eating Indian, the counting goat, and the magician who made a raccoon disappear right before their very eyes.

Easter, leaving but not really heading anywhere in particular, with anger lodged in her throat like a peach pit, marched right past the brigade and then doubled back. She paid her nickel and found herself in the midst of the adults-only midnight ramble, so called because the female performers often stripped out of their clothes.

Easter planted herself between two men. The one to her right was a grizzled old guy who smelled of wet earth. He stood slump-shouldered with his hands shoved deep into the pockets of his pants. His fingers wiggled beneath the material, in search of something Easter was more than sure wasn't coins. The man to her left was long and lanky, with eyes that bulged unnaturally from their sockets, veiling him with a comical jig-a-boo look the white folks caricatured in their daily newspapers.

The members of the three-piece jug band climbed onto the wooden stage and peered put at the audience. A young boy moved along the row of oil lamps carefully igniting their wicks.

Slocum, the short, round, dimple-cheeked proprietor, bounded onto the stage and cast his toothless grin over the crowd before joyfully announcing: "Women hold onto your husbands, men hold tight to your hats, a storm is coming that I guarantee will leave you soaking wet!"

The audience tensed.

"Put your hands together for Mama Raaaaiiiiin!"

The jug band struck up. Fingers covered in thimbles glided down the belly of a washboard, lips blew breath over the ceramic mouth of the whiskey jug, a pick plucked banjo strings, and two pewter spoons angrily conversed. Combined the sounds created music, and Easter began to tap her foot against the sawdust-littered ground. The audience swayed in unison, becoming one living, breathing, rhythmic organ, and then Mama Rain sauntered onto the stage and everyone went still.

Six-foot, red-boned, green-eyed, Geechee girl with close-cut curls the color of straw. She was barefoot and Easter thought that Rain had the prettiest toes she had ever seen. She wore a yellow-feathered boa coiled around her neck.

The music climbed and Rain began to dance, to shimmy and shake, and with every lunge, every hop, the peach pit in Easter's throat began to break apart, to disintegrate into dust. Her mouth went dry and her tongue withered like a tuber left out beneath a blazing, midday sun.

Rain tossed her head seductively to one side, kicked her leg out, pulled it back, rolled her hips, took three dainty steps toward the edge of the stage, and bent over the crowd so that the tops of her breasts peeked above the jewel neckline of the orange silk shift she wore. Mama Rain offered a girlish grin as her shoulders caught the rising melody of the angry pewter spoons. Up in the air now, square with her perfect ears, they began to pump. No one was ready for the next thing that happened. Mama Rain straightened her back, placed her hands on her hips, and with one sudden visceral move she sent her groin forward. The thrust was accentuated by the thundering sound of the band members' heavy boots crashing down onto the stage floor. Two men standing in the front row fell backwards, as if hit by an invisible battering ram. Another thrust and three more men crumbled.

Mama Rain clasped her hands behind her head, curled her mouth into a devious smile, and threw her pelvis forward again, sending five men to their knees and striking Easter with a thirst that she would soon realize a hundred tin cups of water would never satisfy.

When it was all said and done, Rain was soaking wet, the thin shift cleaved to her body, outlining every luscious curve. Easter heard someone whisper, "My Lord," in a sinful and dirty way, and when she looked around to see who had uttered the sacrilegious statement, two sets of eyes were staring right back at her. Easter clamped her hand over her mouth, turned, and fled.

* * *

Easter didn't have a plan or a place to go and so she hung around the brigade grounds, hoping to catch sight of Rain one last time, but she had disappeared and had not reemerged. Easter tried to look as inconspicuous as possible lugging that brown suitcase and dressed in a blue and white dress that made her look like a schoolgirl on the run. She tried to blend, but instead she stuck out like a snowflake in a vat of coal.

"Ain't you got no place to go?"

Easter spun around and found herself eye to eye with Slocum. He considered her, and she took in his blistered lip and heavy eyelashes.

"I need a job." The words jumped out of her mouth and landed on the ground between them. Slocum grunted, slipped his hands behind the bib of the overalls he wore, and rocked back on his heels.

"Oh, really now? What you do?"

Easter shrugged her shoulders. "This and that."

"This and that? Well that's just what we been looking for!" Slocum clapped his hands together and laughed. "Go on home now, ain't nothing here for you." He dismissed her with a quick wave of his hand.

"I—I can cook and clean."

Slocum was walking away. "Can't use you," he threw over his shoulder.

"The hell you can't!" The unmistakable voice boomed behind Easter causing her heart to lurch in her chest. Slocum turned around, an annoyed smirk resting on his lips. "Bennie like to kill me with his cooking, we need a feminine touch. I'm tired of eating lumpy grits and undercooked eggs. Besides, I need someone to attend to me," Rain barked.

"Aww, come on, Rain," Slocum whined, "she just a child—"

"Shut up, she looks pretty grown to me."

Easter was shaking like a leaf.

"Turn around, sugar, lemme get a look at you."

Easter turned around. Rain was standing outside of her tent; the silk robe she wore flapped open revealing her naked body. Easter dropped her eyes.

Rain waltzed over and caught her by the chin. "What's your name, girl?" Her fingers felt like fire against Easter's skin.

"Easter, ma'am," she quaked in a timid voice.

Rain's eyes sparkled. "Easter? That's a real old-timey name. Had a great-aunt named Easter." She cackled and released Easter's chin. "And I ain't no ma'am." She spat, then, "You say you cook and clean?"

"Yes m— I mean yes."

Slocum stepped between the women, wagging his finger in Rain's face. "We ain't pulling in enough money to pay and feed another soul, Rain!"

Rain eyed him menacingly. "Nigger, if you don't get outta my face . . ." Her words trailed off, but the threat hung heavy in the air.

Slocum's hand floated back down to his waist and he stepped cautiously to one side.

"I'll pay her myself, don't you worry about it, you cheap bastard!" Rain snapped, and then turned and started back toward her tent. Easter just stood there, frozen, watching Rain's hips sway beneath the fabric of the robe.

"I done told her 'bout talking to me like that," Slocum grumbled to himself as he kicked at the dirt. "Well what you waiting for, sun-up? Go on, git!"

Easter jumped to life and double-timed to Rain's tent.

"I want you to know right now that I likes women," Rain said as she shrugged her robe off and tossed it onto the cot.

Easter's face unfolded and her stomach clenched. "Not to worry, sugar," Rain laughed, walking over to Easter and pinching her cheek, "you too young for Mama Rain. I like 'em seasoned and you just out of the shell." She laughed again and glided to the opposite side of the tent where she squatted daintily over a cream-colored chamber pot and relieved herself. "You still a virgin?" she asked in a non-chalant tone.

As embarrassed as Easter was by the question, she was more than a little disappointed that Rain wouldn't even consider her as a lover, and then she became angry with herself for wanting such a thing. Easter remained silent.

"Figures." Rain chuckled, gave her bottom a quick shake, and then stood. "Dump it before this entire tent is rank with the stink of piss." She pointed to the pot and after a moment's hesitation Easter hurried to fetch it.

Rain sighed and began to untwine the feather boa from her neck, exposing the keloid scar that looped from one collarbone to the next, resembling a string of brown pearls. Easter's mouth dropped open and then clamped shut again when Rain turned smoldering eyes on her.

"Well what you gonna do, stand there all night holding my piss?"

"Uhm, no ma'am—I mean no," she stammered as she backed out of the tent.

Outside Easter moved quickly and recklessly, causing the piss to slosh over the sides, wetting her hands.
She was disgusted and intrigued. She looked cautiously
around her, and when she saw that no one was watching, she brought her finger to her nose and sniffed. Rain's
piss smelled like gardenias.

Easter would learn that Rain didn't much like men or the
snake that grew down between their legs. It had never
been sweet to her, not from the time she was someone's
sweet little girl, with pigtails, living in Louisiana and
singing in the choir, just eleven years old when her
brother's best friend cornered her in the outhouse and
pressed his forearm against her throat as he rammed
himself inside her, all the while whispering in her ear
that she had it coming. "This is what happens to cock
teasers," he'd said. Afterwards, he called her a "yella
heifer," while he used his shirttail to wipe her blood
from his penis.

Nothing but trouble followed the men that came
later and Hemp Jackson was trouble with a capital T. As
mean and black as the day was long, Hemp had the body
of a bulldog and his right eye was a cloud of cotton. He
chose not to wear an eye patch; he liked the hideous
look that damaged eye graced him with and the fear it
struck in the hearts of men. He claimed that Rain was
the only woman he'd ever loved and gave her a feathered
boa to prove it, which turned out to be a poor substi-
tute for an apology, since he was the one who'd sliced
her neck in the first place. After that there had been a
period of gentleness from a soft-spoken man with kind
eyes. That relationship had produced a son who after

two months Rain had wrapped in a blanket, placed in a basket, and left on the front porch for the soft-spoken man's *wife* to raise. Then she walked right out of that life without even so much as a goodbye to her parents.

Rain didn't like men, which made it easy for her to shake her ass and roll her hips for them. It was the women she loved.

At night, Mama Rain would stretch herself out on her cot, naked except for the boa, and she'd smoke and sip from her flask of white lightning and talk about all the good and bad that had been done to her, the whole while absentmindedly stroking the hairs of the triangle of black hair between her legs. When she caught Easter staring, which was often, she would snort, "This here my cat, I got a right to pet it." And then she would laugh, long and hard, until the laughter became a chuckle and the chuckle became a snore and the empty flask fell down to the sawdust floor.

Show after show and night after night, through downpour and drought, snow and clover, Easter's thirst for Rain swelled and so she reached for her Bible and plunged herself into Scripture, and when that didn't work she turned to her own words. But words—anointed or not—offered no solace and absolutely no quench.

CHAPTER 4

W hat you got there, gal?"
Before Easter could answer, Mama Rain
snatched the notebook from her hands and
held it high above her head. "Some type of diary?"

Easter tried desperately to grab the book, but Rain
was tall and easily kept it out of Easter's reach. "Give it
here!"

Rain laughed, bringing the book toward Easter and
then snatching it away again. *"Give it here,"* Rain mocked.
"You always scribbling in this book. What you writing?"

"It's my business!" Easter snapped as she made yet
another futile leap for the book. "Goddamnit, Rain, you
evil bitch, give it back!"

Rain's palm came across Easter's cheek with so much
force that Easter stumbled backwards until she lost her
footing and fell over, hitting the ground with a hard
thud.

"You watch your tongue, you hear?" Rain's voice was
even, her green eyes narrowed to slits. "You don't ever
call me outta my name."

Easter rubbed her stinging cheek. Rain spent a few
more seconds glaring at her before she returned her
attention to the book. Easter watched as she flipped
through the thin pages, pausing every so often to stare
intently at some word or phrase that had caught her eye.

Easter watched and waited for Rain to see herself in those words in the pages and pages of passages. It was all about Rain, and about the smoldering love Easter had for her. The thirst was there too, blatant and screaming, aching and throbbing. She'd written about it in bold, dark letters. She would have written it in blood if she could have.

Rain finally closed the notebook and gave it one last thoughtful look before tossing it back to Easter.

"So what's it say?"

Easter was bewildered. She'd seen Rain flip through pages of the newspaper as she sat sipping her morning coffee.

"Pardon?"

"I asked you," Rain growled, eyeballing her, "what's it say?"

"Ma'am?" Easter was still confused.

"Goddamnit, don't *ma'am* me!" Rain yelled. "You poking fun at me?"

Easter scurried backwards. "No, I just thought—"

"Yeah, I know what you thought," Rain spat before turning and stomping off.

Her ankle wasn't broken, but it was sprained. The result of a cartwheel gone wrong that sent Rain crashing to the floor, where she lay stunned, her legs splayed wide open. The men in the audience leaned in and groaned with pleasure. Rain was not wearing any underwear.

In her tent, on her cot, between sips of white lightning, she moaned, cussed, and confessed that she was getting too old for that particular type of bullshit. Easter sat at her feet, listening quietly as she gently pressed the chunk of ice onto Rain's bruised skin.

"I'm twenty-eight, you know, an old woman. I ought to be ashamed of myself," she slurred as the flame of the oil lamp danced in her eyes. "I thought I was gonna be famous, but 'stead look at me, dancing and singing for niggers that got a day's worth of dirt under their fingernails." Her words were soaked with disappointment. "My mama probably turning over in her grave."

Easter stared down at Rain's pretty toes.

"What about you? What you wanna be? I know you don't wanna be my maid for the rest of your life, do you?"

Easter shrugged her shoulders. Being with Rain for the rest of her life sounded just fine to her.

"I don't know, haven't really given it much thought."

Rain turned the flask up to her lips and drank deeply. "Stand up, girl, raise your dress and let me see your goods."

Easter turned a crooked eye on her. "What?"

Rain's face went slack. "Well someone's got to do it, might as well be you."

"Do what?"

"For all the writing and reading, you just as dumb as a doornail, ain't you?"

Easter blinked. She was completely lost.

Rain leaned over and peered directly into Easter's wide eyes. "*You* gonna have to take my place in the show until I'm healed."

Easter's jaw dropped.

"Close your mouth, chile, this place full of flies," Rain chuckled.

Easter knew Rain's entire routine by heart, every

hip-swaying, groin-thrusting *boom-chica-boom-chica-boom-boom-boom* move, but that didn't mean that she could pull it off in front of an audience of sex-crazed sharecroppers. And furthermore, Easter didn't have Rain's curves—she was as flat as a board.

Nor did she find it easy to melt into the music, so her attempts at a lascivious bump-and-grind were appalling; in fact, she resembled an epileptic in the throes of a seizure. Comedy was not her intent, but it was the end result and the audience roared with laughter and threw pennies at her feet.

"You a clown, girl! A straight-up fool!" Rain howled when Easter chicken-walked off the stage and into her open arms. "It wasn't me, but it was good!"

"You think so?" Easter was panting.

"Better than good," Rain said, and then pressed her warm lips against Easter's. It happened just that once but Easter would relive it a million times in her dreams.

CHAPTER 5

Ten shows and three towns later, Rain's ankle was healed, good as new. Easter was glad for it, because she was growing tired of playing the fool. The show was working its way down the Savannah River toward Elberton and Easter had fifteen dollars saved. A few more weeks and she figured she'd have enough to hop a train heading somewhere. Maybe, she thought, Rain would come with her.

But Slocum had other plans for Easter, and one evening as she sat eating her dinner of fried snook and boiled potatoes, his bloated, bow-legged shadow fell over her.

"What?"

Slocum grinned as he ceremoniously unfurled the burlap poster he held, revealing a colorful caricature of a cross-eyed, tongue-wagging, knock-kneed Easter.

Rain clapped her hands together and squealed, "You've arrived!"

Arrived where? Easter wondered. The bowels of life? The filthy heels of existence?

That night after the show, the moon sat low and full in the sky as Easter made her way to Rain's tent. This was something she looked forward to all day. It was their time and their time alone in which they did whatever they wanted. Sometimes Easter would sit snug between Rain's legs as Rain used the comb to carve fine lines through Easter's thick hair and then braided it into neat rows. Other times Easter would paint Rain's toenails or knead the knots in her neck until they melted away. Sometimes they'd play Bid Whist or just talk. Always, Easter waited for another kiss, but it never came.

"You never stop scribbling in that notebook, what you scribbling?" Rain had pressed until Easter broke down one day and began to share the stories she'd written about Waycross and the people who lived there. Easter read aloud the tales heavy with Southern dialect and folksy wisdom and Rain's eyes rippled with the images Easter's words created. "You should write a book like dem white folks. You just as good as they are."

That night Easter arrived at Rain's tent as usual, pulled back the canvas flap, and stepped inside. She saw Rain and something else . . . some*one* else, and then the light suddenly disappeared. She thought she'd been struck blind, but then her eyelids suddenly popped open and her shocked gaze collided with Rain's dreamy, moist one. The young girl she'd been kissing blushed, turned her face away, and raised delicate fingers to her lips. Rain caught hold of her wrist and gently eased the girl's hand back down into her lap. "Don't be 'shamed," she cooed lovingly, and Easter almost bit through her tongue.

After that, Easter made up her mind and then made her escape. She crept past the watching horses, the sleeping dog, and the blind prophet who strapped himself to a tree at night because he had fits that sent him stumbling deep into his own black heart. He saw nothing and he saw everything, but Easter never mustered the nerve to place her hands into his; had she done so he would have warned her to avoid the city sweet and told her to point her compass north.

CHAPTER 6

Elberton, Georgia's landscape was littered with gaping holes and the sound of dynamite blasts echoed frequently across the horizon. Most of the men in and around Elberton worked in the quarries, gauging the earth until they struck rock that resembled sparkling river water frozen in time.

Easter had walked all through the night and only stopped to rest when the night sky began to flake away. She caught the scent of strong black coffee and followed it to a shack with a picnic table set out front. A woman was standing in the doorway staring thoughtfully down at the chickens that pecked at the dirt around her feet. When she looked up and saw Easter coming she hollered out, "Got eggs, grits, and hopping John. That's it."

"That's fine," Easter said.

"You look bone-tired, girl." The woman set a battered metal cup down on the table and poured it full with coffee.

Easter stared down into the dark liquid. "You got milk?"

The woman shook her head. "You a li'l early, the boy ain't come with the milk yet. Got sugar though."

"That'll do, I guess," Easter said and waved her hand through the screen of steam rising from the coffee.

The woman walked off and called over her shoulder, "I'm Claudia, by the way."

By the time Easter had finished her meal, two men and a woman carrying a basket of johnny cakes on her head had joined her. They were all heading into Elberton and welcomed Easter into the back of their horse and buggy. The johnny cake she'd bought from the woman was wrapped in newspaper, which was how she came across the ad:

> Colored woman wanted for general housework. Ironing. Some cooking. Fond of children. See Mrs. S. Comolli at 115 Heard Street between 2PM and 4PM.

115 Heard Street loomed over a sweeping emerald lawn that was dotted with crab apple trees. It was an ostentatious structure, carved out of stone with columns and floor-to-ceiling windows. The Spanish-tiled roof glowed ginger beneath the sun.

Easter's body felt condemned by the time she climbed down off of that buggy. Her knees popped and creaked as she walked around to the side of the house and scaled the steps. When she caught sight of her reflection in the shiny glass pane of the window, she didn't recognize the woman looking back at her. Her hair was a mess and her clothes were disheveled. Who in the world would hire someone who looked like they'd walked across the state? Easter quickly did the best she could with her hair, tucked her blouse tight behind the waistband of her skirt, and then raised the bronze knocker and allowed it to fall. A few moments later a dark, generous-sized woman opened the door. She winced when she saw Easter standing there—as if the very sight of her caused her pain.

"Yes?"

Fatigue swooped down on Easter and even though her eyes were wide open, she felt herself begin to dream.

"Are you lost, gal?"

Easter swayed, then raised the newspaper and declared, "I'm here about the job."

The woman considered her. "You got fever," she ventured, taking a cautious step back and raising a cupped hand over her nose.

"No, I been walking most of the day. I guess I'm just worn out."

The woman eyed her. "You from 'round here?"

"No ma'am, I'm from Waycross."

The woman's eyes bulged. "You walk all the way from Waycross!"

Easter laughed, turned, and pointed in the direction she'd come from. "No ma'am, just from . . ." She trailed off; the image of Rain's dewy eyes and sweet face swam in her vision and Easter felt her heart break apart again. She swallowed, changed direction, and said, "The job still available?"

Olivia Comolli was olive-colored and wore her golden tresses piled in a loose bun on top of her head.

"Easter Bartlett?"

"Yes ma'am," Easter replied when the woman called her name for the third time.

"Unique name. Easter." The woman seemed to enjoy the name against her tongue.

"Yes ma'am."

Olivia led Easter into an immense room filled with granite podiums that held marble busts of significant-looking men. The walls were covered in fabric the color of blood and embossed with golden leaves. Oil paintings propped on brass easels depicted everything from a simple vase filled with weeping flowers to bird dogs and their grim-eyed owners.

After Olivia interviewed Easter, she leaned back and considered her for a long moment before she said, "You speak different from the other Negro women I employ here. You have education, yes?"

"Yes ma'am, I do."

"Well," Olivia said, her voice ringing with excitement, "we have just lost our Negro school teacher and I think you would be the perfect replacement."

The Negro part of Elberton was called Sweet City and Easter arrived with some high school, learning the knowledge she'd obtained from her beloved books, and a hand-written letter of introduction from one of the most respected women in Elberton.

"Ask for Mrs. Abigail at this address," Olivia had said as she scribbled the address down on a piece of linen stationery, "she'll rent you a room." Olivia's hand stopped moving and she looked up at Easter. Her eyes rolled over her as if seeing her for the first time. "You do have money, don't you?"

"Yes ma'am."

A look of relief spread across Olivia's face. "Good." She handed Easter the paper. "It's about an hour down the road."

Easter started toward Sweet City beneath a relentless sun. Five minutes into her journey she knew she wouldn't make it and so stepped off the road and found a cool space beneath a tree. She spread her nightgown over the grass and used the suitcase as a pillow and in no time was fast asleep. When she woke, the loons were crooning.

The rooming house catered to Negroes but was owned by whites. The tenants were housed Oreo-cookie style—young Negro women on the top floor, the white landlord and his wife in the middle, and elderly Negro men on the first floor. This living arrangement concerned the whites in Elberton and they shared their concerns with the owners. *Niggers on the first floor . . . The first floor is your first line of defense and you done gone and assigned the enemy to guard your front door!*

Easter wondered too, but when she met the men, it was immediately clear that any threat either of them ever presented had been beat out of them, poured, blended, and baked into humble pie decades earlier. The only contest they still possessed was for the affections of the owners and even that they had to share with the family dog.

Easter's room was cozy and newly wallpapered, with a bay window. There was a small writing desk, an even smaller closet, and a full-sized bed with squeaky springs. She had her books, her space, and time to breathe, feel, think, and write. Who knew contentment had been hiding in a place called Sweet City?

The school was a one-room shack that sat a few yards away from the Mission Springs AME Church. The air inside the school was hot, sticky, and heavy with the scent of chalk and old books. The minister instructed her that she would be teaching children ranging in age from six to seventeen.

As the children filed in Easter carefully picked over their faces, and was quick to pinpoint the troublemakers, the slackers, the enthusiasts, and the meek. She offered a welcoming smile, moved to pull the door shut, and almost collided head-on with a latecomer whose face was as angelic as a cherub.

"'Scuse me, ma'am," he said as he scurried around her.

She watched him move toward a seat in the last row and decided that he was at least eighteen if he was a day. Eighteen seemed right because of his gait and the confidence he wore tight around his waist like a belt belonging to a man twice his age. He settled himself into the chair, leaned back, folded his thin, muscular arms across his chest, and smirked at her.

He smirked at her and all four walls of that room collapsed. He smirked and the earth yawned and all but the two of them slipped down its grainy throat. Easter felt her mouth go dry and she reached for the water glass and brought it carefully to her lips. As she drank Easter wondered what in the world was wrong with her, because she was sure she'd left that thirst miles behind her, somewhere along the banks of the Savannah River.

Regaining her composure, she set the glass back down on the desk and began the morning roll call.

"John Appleby?"

"Here."

"April Botwin?"

"Here."

Easter moved slowly down the list of names, aware of the cherub's eyes boring into her. She crossed and uncrossed her legs, and felt her tongue begin to wither behind her teeth. By the time she reached *his* name, her voice had dropped to a hoarse whisper and it tumbled out in a gale of dust.

"Getty Wisdom?"

"Present."

Have you ever heard a sweeter-sounding name?

Week in and week out she covered penmanship, arithmetic, *The Mayflower*, Washington's cherry tree, and honest Abe. She tended to scabbed knees, knotted lose shoelaces, broke up scuffles, read her books, and wrote her stories. When she was alone in her room she thought about Getty and admonished herself in soft whispers. "Shoot girl, you done lost your damn mind." Standing before the mirror she'd wave her hand at her reflection and ask, "What he see in you? He just a—"

She would stop herself from saying that he was just a child. She'd convinced herself that if she didn't say it . . . if she didn't even think it, then it couldn't be true.

Her mirrored reflection smiled back at her and said, *He gotta be eighteen if he's a day.*

Harvest time came and the class thinned. All hands were needed at home, Getty Wisdom's included. Just the littlest ones remained and Easter's mood turned gray.

Getty Wisdom.

She would open a book to read and his name jumped out from between the lines of the story.

Getty Wisdom.

When she sat down to write, it was his name that spilled from her fountain pen.

Getty Wisdom.

When the harvest season came to an end, Easter was giddy with excitement and went out and bought herself a new pair of nylons and made sure that the scented powder she'd dusted her neck with was visible above the collar of her blouse. She was sitting at her desk looking expectantly at the doorway when he finally appeared, and her heart stopped. He was taller than she remembered, his arms were bigger, his neck wider. He smelled of fresh-turned earth and was scrubbed so clean he shined. He took his seat and gave her that same look he had the first time they laid eyes on one another, and just like that their dance resumed. Her heart came to life again and the thumping sound transformed into a throbbing, aching thing that was quickly inching south.

Easter pressed her knees tightly together and tried hard to think about something else, something other than him, but a lot of good it did because all she got for her effort were bruised knees.

And so it became stunningly clear to Easter that if she didn't get out of Sweet City—and quick—she would buckle under the weight of her desires, so she claimed fever, dismissed the class, and ran home beneath a fat lazy sun.

The suitcase lay open on the bed, with her best dress, a blouse, and a skirt neatly folded inside. She had a brassiere in one hand and a hairbrush in the other when the knock came to her bedroom door. Easter yanked it open and there he was, long, lean, and glistening.

"Ma'am, you left this behind," Getty's mouth said, but his eyes whispered something different.

He held her notebook out to her and when she reached to take it her hand caught hold of his wrist and she pulled him into her and pressed her lips against his. His nectar was intoxicating and Easter knew that she was lost. They stumbled clumsily to the bed and as they worked to free her from her brassiere and him from his trousers, she told herself that she would never again become that dried tuber, that first autumn leaf—that this time she would toss herself in wholly and completely as if Getty meant survival itself and she would drink from his cup until her passion floated. She would drink until she burst.

He buried himself inside her and Easter became a bud in spring. He lifted her legs and placed them over his shoulders and she blossomed and vainly preened for him, for the horsefly that watched from the wall, and the humming bird fluttering outside the open window.

Afterwards, they lay very, very still and before Getty drifted off to sleep he was aware of many things—the damp smell of their bodies, the darkness, her chin resting in the indented space beneath his Adam's apple, and the heaviness of her leg against his hip bone. If he had remained awake just a few seconds longer he would have seen Easter's eyes moving over him, claiming every young inch of him, and he would have felt her arms become clutching roots and his ears would have buzzed with the sound of her heart beating out one steady song: *gettywisdom, gettywisdom, gettywisdom* . . .

* * *

They carried on like that through autumn, first frost, winter, and straight into the madness of March. The lie she told when he stole from her room that first magical night had to do with books and study. The landlord's wife, Miss Abigail, scrunched her face up and Easter did not miss the doubt glowing in her blanched cheeks, so she kept her distance from Getty for a week and waited for the talk, but none came her way and people did not turn to salt when they looked at her.

And so they began to meet in out-of-the-way places.

When the weather permitted, a favorite spot was along the riverbank beneath a cluster of tree roots that formed a cave. There in the darkness she fed him scuppernongs and licked the sweet juice from his lips while they made love. Another place was a barn, long abandoned by its owner, where the sky seeped between the rotting wooden rafters and the air still held the scent of the young mares that once lived there. When the nights turned frigid, Easter borrowed a truck from one of the old roomers; they drove two towns away, parked off of a rarely traveled road, and she climbed on top of Getty and indulged herself while the engine grumbled angrily beneath the battered red hood of the cab and the steering wheel pressed half moon–shaped welts into the small of her back.

By April, though, he had milk in his eyes.

Sara Lee.

She was beyond high yellow, closer to alabaster in color, with a thick tail of black hair that dangled down her back. Easter imagined its weightiness and visualized how she would coil the braid around Sara Lee's pretty little neck and choke the light out of her eyes.

In class, Sara Lee sat beside Getty and it was all he could do to keep from staring at her. During recess he showed himself up, strutting like a cock and grinning like a minstrel-show buffoon. Easter watched the display and tiny explosions went off in her chest.

Getty began walking Sara Lee home from school, carrying her books in the crook of his arm—where Easter's head used to lay.

Two, three, and then five weeks went by and Getty avoided Easter's advances and pretended not to see the little notes she left between the pages of his copy of *The Adventures of Huckleberry Finn*.

Easter's anger festered and her jealousy turned into a mite beneath her skin that kept her up at night pacing the floors and clawing at her flesh.

Well it looks *like my handwriting,* she thought, *but it definitely isn't. I don't write my* e *that way, or my* s *or my* a.

The letter was an accumulation of her unraveling that had started on the school day when Easter looked down to find that she was wearing one brown shoe and one black shoe. And there was that Wednesday when she was snatched out of her sleep by a loud banging at her door. When she opened it, she was met with the fretful face of Miss Abigail.

"The minister sent word to check on you. Are you sick?"

"No," Easter responded, dragging a hand through her unkempt hair.

"Then why," the old woman asked as she peered over Easter's shoulder into the shuttered room, "are you not at school today?"

Easter yawned, "Because it's Saturday." Her voice dripped with annoyance.

The woman bristled and snapped, "No, it's Wednesday."

Easter peered down at the letter again.

Getty,

> *What of the love you whispered in my ear when you were buried deep inside of me? Was that a lie? Or has that bright bitch cast a spell on you? I beg you, meet me at our place by the river so that we can talk.*
>
> *I love you.*

Minister Tuck scratched the bald spot at the center of his head with one hand and used the other to fish his handkerchief out of the breast pocket of his jacket. He dabbed the cloth against his nose.

"You have been an exemplary teacher, Miss Bartlett, but as of late . . ." His words dropped away as he attended to his nose.

Easter waited.

"You seem to be distracted. But this . . ." Again his words faded, his face flushed scarlet, and he seemed to look to Easter to finish his thought. When she offered no help, he started again, dropping his voice an octave. "This is a Christian school, Miss Bartlett, and this," he said, tapping his finger angrily against the letter, "is inappropriate. I would have to report it to the authorities. He is a child, you know, just fifteen years old."

No, Easter did not know, and her head snapped up in surprise and disbelief. The reaction was telling. Minister Tuck fell back into his chair as if he'd been shot in the heart.

"Of . . . of course you would have to report it if I'd written it, but I didn't," Easter stammered. "I'm insulted that you would think me capable of such a thing." Easter stood up. "It's a joke. A childish prank," she continued, her hands gripping the edge of the desk.

Minister Tuck was a man of God, a man of the cloth, but he was still a man, an imperfect being, and he'd had his waywardness, oh yes, his flesh had been weak. But he was a man, and certain behaviors were expected of men. But a woman?

Minister Tuck picked up the letter and shook it at Easter. "People have seen you two *together*."

Who? she wanted to ask. They'd been careful. Very careful.

"Yes," Easter barked and straightened her back. "I have tutored him on occasion."

"Watch your tone, Miss Bartlett. You need to tread lightly."

"You tread lightly, sir!" Easter bellowed back at him.

Tuck was stunned and reeled back in his chair. Easter's face contorted with rage. She looked like a trapped animal and he had no doubt that she would pounce on him if he made any sudden moves. So they glared at one another, each waiting for the other to fold, and then finally Easter did and the anger whistled out of her.

Tuck slowly raised his hand and wrapped his fingers around the small silver cross that hung around his neck. Easter cleared her throat, smoothed the pleats of her dress, and calmly eased herself down into the chair.

Then she asked, "Where did you get this letter?"

She knew it had to be the girl. Sara Lee had prob-ably fished it from his pocket during some childish act of foreplay.

Tuck squeezed the cross until the prongs cut into his palm and said, "The boy gave it to me."

CHAPTER 7

Praise the Lord if it ain't Easter Bartlett!" Their reintroduction took place in the colored car of the Atlantic Coast Line headed to Virginia. Easter had given the chestnut-brown woman a blank look. The eyes had seemed familiar, but the sophisticated hairstyle and dapper attire had thrown her.

"C'mon now," the woman said as she wiggled her behind into the seat beside Easter. "It's me, Madeline! Don't be that way. We go too far back for you not to remember me."

Easter looked harder.

The woman grinned, proudly patted her bobbed hair, and licked her painted lips before she curled her palm around her mouth, leaned close to Easter's ear, and whispered, "Mattie Mae Dawkins, from down home Waycross, girl!"

Easter's neck snapped. "For real?"

Mattie Mae Dawkins was calling herself Madeline now, and Easter supposed it was the right thing to do because she didn't look much like the tenant farmer's daughter Easter had known her to be.

Mattie Mae's grin spread and she bubbled, "Sure nuff."

"Why did you change your name?"

Madeline huffed, "Mattie Mae is country, and I'm a city girl now."

"What city would that be?"

Madeline's face unstitched and her fizzle went flat. "Why, New York City!" she said, as if that was the only city in the country or even the world.

"Oh."

Madeline was returning to New York from Florida, where she'd spent two weeks with her sister and new-born nephew. She was heading back to Harlem, where she had a job in a beauty shop and a room in a row house.

Easter smiled inwardly. If she'd had any doubts about this woman being the former Mattie Mae Dawkins, the not-so-new Madeline had put them to rest. The rambling, the babbling, endless waves of words was vintage Mattie Mae. Easter was ecstatic to have her talking a mile a minute in her ear. Madeline reminded her of home and Easter was suddenly awash with nostalgia. And then the good feeling cracked when Madeline said, "Heard about your mama. Sorry . . ."

She didn't mention Rlizbeth and Easter was thankful. The dead were better off than the living, so Easter knew her mother was fine. But she'd run off and left Rlizbeth in that house with that man who used to be her father and his new wife. Every day she tried not to think about that, and every day she failed.

"Thank you," Easter said and patted Madeline's knee.

The steel wheels of the train churned, streaking them past trees, homes, and children lined alongside the tracks, bearing teeth and pink gums as they hopped in place and waved gleefully at the passengers.

"So, where you headed?" Madeline asked.

"Richmond."

"Richmond? I didn't know you had people there."

Easter didn't have a soul there. But she'd purchased a ticket that would take her to the end of the line and the end of the line was Richmond, Virginia. Seemed as good a place as any.

"I don't."

Madeline frowned. "Well, why in the world you going there then? You got a job waiting for you?"

Easter shook her head.

"I don't understand."

She didn't understand either. "Just some place new I guess."

Madeline brightened. "Like an adventure?"

Easter's brow knitted. That was the other thing about Mattie Mae–now–Madeline, she was light and airy in her head with a strong tendency toward childishness.

"Yes, something like that I suppose."

"I love adventures," Madeline squealed, and clapped her hands together like a four-year-old before setting off on a story: "When I first went to New York . . ."

Easter rested her head against the window and allowed Madeline's words to wash over her.

The train pulled into Richmond under a heavy sky. The platform was wet and the air moist. Children ran up and down the platform stomping their feet in the puddles of water the afternoon showers had left behind. Porters buzzed busily, but kept their heads lowered, careful not to make direct eye contact with the men who'd been sent down from Detroit to recruit workers for the Ford Motor Company. Ford was paying his employees five dollars a day and Southern states found their cheap labor streaming out of their towns and cities as quickly as sand through a sieve.

Some recruiters had been abducted and beaten. But Ford just sent more in their place and so the railroad officials had begun to systematically prohibit the sale of northbound tickets to Negroes or inflate the price to such an exorbitant level that it became unaffordable.

Easter followed Madeline into the colored waiting area. She'd promised to sit with her until the train headed to New York arrived. They bought two oranges, squeezed into a space on a long, wooden bench, and quietly worked at peeling the thick skin from the fruit.

"I really think you should come with me to New York," Madeline suggested for the umpteenth time. "I can get you a job at the hair salon and I can't see my landlady minding you staying with me until you got your own place."

Easter bit into the wedge of fruit and the sweet juice coated the inside of her cheek. She didn't have an excuse not to go and couldn't rationalize why she felt so resistant to the idea.

"Easter, it's not like anyplace you've ever been before."

Easter laughed to herself. Where had Madeline been that allowed her to make such a grand statement? Waycross, Georgia and Jacksonville, Florida, that's it.

Madeline pressed, "You ain't got nobody here; at

least in New York you'd have me and my aunt Minnie in the Bronx."

Easter chuckled, "She still make ambrosia?"

Madeline nodded and her face brightened. She was wearing Easter down. "Oh, say you'll come," she whined. "If you don't like it you can always leave."

Easter thought about it for a moment. "Okay."

The conductor rang his bell and hollered, "All aboard!" The whistle sounded and the train huffed great billowing clouds of steam. Easter clutched her ticket tightly in her hand. She was headed to New York. A quiet excitement percolated in her stomach and she felt a smile light on her lips. When the nose of the train edged across the border between Maryland and Pennsylvania, a young, dark porter appeared and unceremoniously removed the tin sign above the doorway that stated, *COLORED*.

The car exploded in applause and hearty whoops went up into the air. Couples kissed one another full on the lips. Parents grabbed hold of their children and squeezed. Easter felt something lift off of her shoulders and her leg began to bounce with anticipation.

With the Mason-Dixon line behind them, the train barreled at a reckless speed toward New York.

BOOK II

UP SOUTH

CHAPTER 8

Nothing in the world could have prepared her—not Madeline's descriptions, not anything she'd read in her beloved books, not even what her imagination had conjured up over the years.

Pennsylvania Station was brimming with people all in motion. The red caps moved fluidly between the masses as if they themselves traveled along an invisible track.

"Porter, ma'am? Porter, sir?"

Madeline clasped Easter by the hand, dragging her swiftly along behind her. "Keep up, girl. If I lose you in this crowd we'll never find each other!"

Easter's mind whirled and she realized that she was panting—sights, sounds, and the beautiful chaos of it all had literally snatched her breath away.

In the subway Easter and Madeline stood on the platform amidst dozens—no, hundreds—of other people of a variety of colors. Easter stared down the dark throat of the tunnel and saw a pair of dim eyes peering back at her. As the train chugged closer its eyes brightened and Easter's body went still. The train leapt into the station with a thunderous growling wind that whipped Easter's hair into her eyes.

They packed in.

The fans spun noisily above their heads as the passengers were swept along through the eerie darkness of the tunnels. A stop and more people piled in. Bodies pressed against the doors and each other. When the train began to scale an invisible incline, passengers planted their feet and tightened their grip on the poles and dangling leather straps. Up, up, up they went. Easter imagined that they were climbing into the sky, into the heavens. They climbed up and into glittering sunlight. The train came to a halt, the door slid open revealing a black and white sign: *135th Street.*

Madeline nudged her toward the open door and whispered, "This is Harlem."

The air up there, up south, up in Harlem, was sticky sweet and peppered with perfume, sweat, sex, curry, salt meat, sautéed chicken livers, and fresh baked breads. The streets teamed with automobiles, streetcars, and horse-drawn wagons. Brick buildings lined the sidewalks like soldiers. On the street corners young boys cried, "Extra! Extra! Read all about it!" An elderly woman beckoned people over to peruse her wagon packed with pots and pans, and a legless man stretched out on a slab of wood fitted with wheels used his hands like fish fins and swam through the streets begging for nickels.

Easter's ears rang with the city sounds, the familiar twang of Southern tongues and the Northern strum that Madeline had adopted. They made a stop at a fruit cart and while Madeline fretted over the peaches, Easter was spirited away by the singsong language of a dark and gleaming West Indian couple. Mesmerized, she found herself walking alongside them, gawking like a child.

"Eh-eh," the woman sounded, and pressed her purse

firmly against her breast when she caught Easter staring.

Easter continued to stare, waiting for one or both of them to spout another beautiful word, but the woman just rolled her eyes and hastened her pace. The man, though, offered a broad smile filled with teeth as white as piano keys.

She and Madeline turned down East 133rd Street, which was a block in stark contrast to the frenzy of Lenox Avenue. Shaded and quiet, the street was lined with brownstone homes, with brass door handles that twinkled in the late-day sun.

As they walked Madeline raised her hand in greeting and called out to neighbors who watched from their front yards.

"Afternoon, Miss Trundle."

"Hey, girl, yeah, I'm back. You ain't working today? Oh, this here is my friend Easter."

"Mr. Carson, your cat feeling any better?"

"Don't get no ideas, Charlie, I already done warned her about the likes of you!"

Number 17 was a narrow brownstone home that sat between a redbrick horse stable and an identical brownstone. The slender hall held a stairway that spiraled up to the third floor. The wood floors creaked beneath their feet and the scent of lemon oil lingered in the air. Madeline knocked on the closed pocket door. When no response came she walked to the end of the hallway, leaned girlishly over the banister, and called down: "Miss Chappo?"

"Yes?"

"It's Madeline."

"Yes?"

"Can you come up here, please? I'd like to ask you something."

There was a long silence and then, "You can come down."

The garden level was comprised of a cozy front bedroom with a fireplace and shuttered windows. The kitchen sat at the back. Beyond that was a bathroom and cold storage shed that led out into a rectangular yard.

"Miss Chappo, this is my friend from back home, Easter Bartlett."

Chappo Elliott stood barely five feet tall, with a thick mass of reddish-brown hair that had been separated and plaited into four braids. Her light complexion was splattered with freckles. Georgia born and raised, she'd lived in Kentucky for eight years before moving to Harlem with her husband and son.

Chappo said, "Nice to meet-cha."

Madeline began to plead Easter's case and Chappo listened as she floured whiting and chicken legs for frying. It was Friday and she lived just a block away from the cabarets of Jungle Alley. In a few hours, black and white alike would be lined up outside of her house to purchase her fifty-cent food plates.

Madeline rambled on and Chappo nodded and smiled where she was supposed to, her eyes swinging between Madeline and Easter, who Chappo decided was wearing an unmistakable glow. If Madeline was going to ask what Chappo thought she was going to ask, the answer would have to be no.

Five women in one house?

That was entirely too much pussy under one roof and she didn't want to dangle additional temptation in front of her husband. She'd only just replaced her rolling pin after using it to bash him across the head when she caught him peering up the dress of one of the tenants as she climbed the stairs. Allowing Easter to move in—as plain and as waifish as she was—would still be a problem, because plain or not she still had a *split* and her husband was still the man he was and Chappo didn't want to have to ruin yet another rolling pin.

And besides, her twelve-year-old son was coming into season so technically that would be *two* heads to clobber. And whether this girl knew it or not, she was with child and Chappo didn't do babies—and so the answer would have to be absolutely, positively no.

But when Madeline said that Easter could pay three weeks up front, the freckles across Chappo's face started dancing. She was a money-hungry woman and she knew it wasn't the Christian way, but God knew her heart and that's all that mattered.

"How long you expectin' to stay?"

Easter muttered something and Chappo cocked an ear in her direction. "Say again?"

Easter spoke up. "Just until I get a place of my own."

What kind of answer was that? *Just until I get a place of my own.* That could take weeks, months, and by then the girl would be close to her time—well, if she decided to keep it. Of course, if she decided to go the other way Chappo could certainly help her out with that, for a fee.

"Well I got rules here. I don't 'low no mens runnin' in and outta my house. You can have a gentleman caller every now and then, but you got to keep company in the front parlor. You pay your rent every Monday, I don't wanna hear no 'scuses. Understand?"

"Yessum," Easter agreed.

The women turned to leave, but Chappo called out, "Wait a minute, I gotta ask you something."

"Ma'am?"

"Do you love Jesus?"

"Yes ma'am, I do."

Madeline's room was larger than the other three on the top floor and overlooked 133rd Street. That first night, after a meal of Chappo's fried chicken and potato salad, the two friends climbed into the double-sized Murphy bed and tucked the sheet tight beneath their chins. Madeline drifted quickly into slumber, but Easter was too excited to sleep and lay awake for most of the night, clapping her heels together, her ears anxiously tuned into Harlem's nocturnal sounds: the soft braying of the horses in the next door stable, the baritone and sopranos belting their hearts out in a distant cabaret, a woman passionately calling out to her husband. Easter inhaled, filling her nostrils with the mixed scents of Madeline's hair, the dizzying aroma of the cheap perfume worn by the girl in the next room, and the cinnamon that Chappo had set to boil to mask the scent of the cooking fish.

Soon her eyes became heavy and she fell asleep and dreamed she was dancing on the moon.

CHAPTER 9

Seventeen East 133rd Street already had the sounds—creaking floorboards, the rattle of the skylight when the wind blew off the Harlem River. In the winter the house groaned like an arthritic man and the furnace coughed in sympathy.

Chappo had brought the smells—iodoform, asafetida, and turpentine, along with herbs kept in clear jars, all varieties of dried animal feces, fried cow tongue, cured alligator tail, and pickled eel. There was magic in those jars for they held remedies for the hiccups, stomach worms, skin rashes, thinning hair, blurry vision, wanton women, no-account men, and unwanted babies.

Chappo was doing the work her mother and grandmother had done before her, God's work—at least the work he didn't have time to do himself.

A month after Easter arrived on Chappo's doorstep, she fainted dead away at Bibb's Hair Shop, where Madeline had gotten her a job as a wash girl. Madeline brought her home and put her in bed. After which she went downstairs and inquired if Chappo might have something she could whip up for her friend who wasn't feeling herself.

Chappo hummed in her throat and instructed Madeline to stay in the kitchen and keep an eye on the pot of hog maws she was cooking.

Upstairs, she didn't bother to knock, so when Easter opened her eyes Chappo was standing over her.

"Ma'am?" Easter hardly had strength enough to lift her head.

Chappo was not one to mince words, so she got straight to the point. "Your friend know you pregnant?"

Goddamit, Easter thought, she didn't even know herself until three days ago.

"No ma'am."

"What are your intentions?"

She hadn't really thought about it.

"I ain't judging you. I ain't gonna call you loose or nothing like that. All I'm going to say is this: the devil's sneaky and he's busy."

Chappo stopped and watched Easter's face for any change. Someone's muffled giggles penetrated the wall and Chappo flung an exasperated look in that direction.

"I like you, Easter, you pay your rent on time, you quiet and respectful, but I can't let you have no baby here. If I 'low that, the rest of these girls up here will feel they could do the same, you hearing me?"

Easter nodded.

Chappo sat down onto the edge of the bed. The coils squealed. "If you decide you don't want it, I can help you with that," she whispered.

Easter suspected as much. She'd seen the women coming and going. Some arrived alone, meek as lambs, throwing nervous glances over their shoulders before scurrying through the door. Others came with men who waited outside, pacing the sidewalk, smoking one ciga-rette after another. Sometimes they rolled their sleeves to their elbows and played stickball with the neighborhood kids until their women emerged, hunched over and weeping. Easter never imagined that she could be one of those women.

Chappo patted her thigh. "You just think about it and let me know. But don't wait too long."

She stood to leave, but Easter caught her by the wrist and asked, "When can we do it?"

Two days later she was in the basement of number 17, flat on her back with her knees pointing toward the ceiling.

"Just relax, baby, it'll be over before you know it," Chappo said as she brought the bottle of ether to Easter's nose. Easter inhaled twice before she was overcome with a sense of weightlessness. She giggled when Chappo pulled her legs apart.

"This is going to hurt a little," Chappo warned before slipping the thin metal rod up into Easter's vagina and piercing her womb.

Easter cried out and tried to clamp her legs shut, but the ether had made her weak and Chappo's meaty hand was strong. She pushed the rod deeper and Easter called out for her mother.

"Hold on," Chappo whispered as she removed the instrument, turned it around, and inserted the hooked end. She gave it a brutal yank, which ripped the gestational sac clean from Easter's womb.

Easter shot straight up, opened her mouth, screamed, and then passed out.

CHAPTER 10

The men were always on that corner as if they were spawned from the cement. Or maybe they were who the ironworker had dreamed of when he poured the molten metal into the cast and formed the long, dark leg of the streetlamp. When the radical thinkers weren't on that corner perched atop their stepladders and soapboxes like great ibises, spouting fire, fury, and awareness, the others were there, trampling over the morning sunlight and the three-o'clock shadow. They abandoned the corner only after evening fell and the moon tipped the big dipper, splattering the sky with stars.

Their moods determined how they would approach the women. When the weather was fair and the sky like glass above their heads, they hooted and hollered out, "Lovely, not even a smile? Oooh, you're breaking my heart!" On crisp days they bowed low and made great sweeping gestures with their hands. For attention one man was fond of jumping high into the air, bringing the heels of his Sunday shoes together in a resounding *click*, *click*.

The good girls tried their best to remain good and hid their smiles behind their hands as they hurried off in the opposite direction.

As far as the men were concerned, 135th Street and

Lenox Avenue was Eden. Three beauty shops within spitting distance of each other meant droves and droves of beautiful women coming and going from ten in the morning till ten at night, Tuesday through Saturday. Many a match had been made between a wash-and-rinse girl and corner boy. But Easter couldn't be bothered with any of them. Her mind was set, she said, on something and someone higher.

"Who," Madeline teased, "God?"

God appeared on that very corner on a cold December night. He stood out not only because he stood tall, nearly six-five, but because in direct sunlight his ebony skin glistened Prussian blue. In the cane fields of Barbados where he'd once labored, the men clamored to work alongside him. Colin Gibbs, they said, provided cool shade.

In 1908, Colin Gibbs packed a canvas bag with the few belongings he owned, along with four salt breads, three roasted pigtails, two cheese cutters, four bananas, two mangos, five limes, and one golden apple. He hoisted his deck chair over his shoulder, planted a kiss on his mother's cheek, and bade her goodbye as he stepped from the small chattel house and joined the stream of men marching out of Pie Corner, St. Lucy. They were all headed to Carlisle Bay, where they boarded the vessel *Thames* and sailed for six days and nights to Colón, Panama.

Three hundred heartbeats sounded above the crashing waves of the bay as the *Thames* moved slowly out into open water. From the beach, his mother stood teary-eyed watching the ship until it disappeared over the horizon.

Back then, Panama had been the land of milk and

honey. Thousands of Caribbean men left their island homes in search of work on the Panama Canal. But when the S.S. *Thames* brought itself to a shuddering stop, Colin cast his eyes over the thick jungle that had been beaten back from the shore with hatchets and machetes and thoughts of neither milk nor honey sprung to mind. Undaunted, he adjusted the shoulder strap of his canvas bag, tightened his grip on the leg of the deck chair, and joined the line of disembarking contract workers.

"Goddamn if you don't look like Babe the Blue Ox!" the man they called Louisville loudly announced, then tilted his head back and sounded a long, shrill whistle. "You know that story, boy? 'Paul Bunyan and Babe the Blue Ox?'"

Colin remained quiet and brought his eyes level with the big-bellied white man who sat behind a wooden table, shaded by a canvas sail. He'd heard stories of white Americans and how they dealt with their blacks. But Colin was no Yankee nigger; he was a British subject.

"I'm going to call you Ox. How you like that?" Louisville folded his arms across his chest and grinned.

Colin dug into the pocket of his khakis and pulled out a slip of paper, which he presented to Louisville. The man stared at the contract, cleared his throat, and hocked a large glob of saliva over the table. It landed in the grayish sand an inch from Colin's shoe.

"What you got to say about that, Ox?"

A man in line behind Colin grumbled, "Wat de rasshole this foolishness gwan here?"

Colin took a mighty breath, placed the paper down on the table, and said, "My name is Colin. Colin Gibbs."

"Louisville, get to moving, the men are becoming restless," a higher-up shouted over.

Louisville snatched the paper from the table. "I'd like to take you back to Kentucky with me," he sneered wickedly. "You know what we do to niggers in Kentucky?"

Colin held his gaze.

"In Kentucky we make big buck niggers like yourself get down on all fours and we fit them with yokes and put them out to plow."

Colin's face remained placid.

"I got just the yoke for you, boy," Louisville continued. "Pretty too, made it myself out of sassafras." And with that he jerked his thumb toward a wagon that held a group of men sitting shoulder to shoulder, simmering beneath the scorching Panama sun. "Get outta my sight!"

Colin's first weeks in Panama were spent on a dredge crew shoveling through the Culebra Cut. Months later, his back strapped with a large metal urn filled with crude oil, he walked twelve hours a day scouring acres and acres of land for pools of mosquito larvae–infested water.

He and the other Negroes were paid in silver. The whites were paid in gold. Colin worked extra hard, took no days off, and often sold his meal tickets to the stout men who never seemed to get their fill. He ignored his hunger, his aching muscles, and the names the Panamanians called him: Chumbo!

He ignored the heat, the mosquitoes, the dead bodies that were carried out of the jungle on stretchers, and the names the whites called him: Nigger!

He ignored it all and sent most of his money home

to his mother. He did not spend a shilling on liquor or women and when the other men asked him why, he said, "Me going to buy myself a little house with a shop and land. Me going to raise pigs for slaughter and then me going to America."

"For true?" the men cried facetiously.

"Yeah man, for true."

Madeline and Easter stood on the corner of 135th Street and Lenox Avenue amidst a throng of people who'd gathered to hear Marcus Garvey, the founder of the Universal Negro Improvement Association, speak. The subject that evening was Negro laborers in Caruthersville, Missouri, who over the past month had been threatened and intimidated by whites fearful of losing their jobs to the influx of Negroes pouring into the area.

Marcus Garvey's dark skin glowed against the gray brick of the building behind him. His jowls trembled and his eyes gleamed like polished onyx. A supreme orator, the man who the people in Harlem had dubbed "Black Moses," possessed the vigor and vehemence of a Southern Baptist minister.

Easter's eyes scanned the crowd and she could not spy one skeptic amongst them—except for the pale and ominous faces of the police officers stationed around the perimeter of the crowd.

Marcus's eyes ranged angrily over his audience as he cried, "Ambrose Young, a Negro, appealed for protection after he had received several warnings. 'Nigger, get to hell out of here. This is a white man's country,' was one notice delivered by five hooded men, Young said. 'The next night I found another note on my front porch, weighted down with a cartridge box. It said: *Nigger, if you can't read, run. If you can't run, you're as good as dead.*

"This bit of news is not broadcast; it is copied from one of the papers in New York. It is a significant bit of news. In thirty days, two thousand Negroes were driven out of a certain section of the country."

The audience grumbled, a few shouted, two women fought their way through the wall of people and went wailing into the autumn night.

"Once upon a time the Negro would have been welcome to do farm work because no white man wanted that job, but now we are gradually reaching the point where even the most menial job the white man finds that he has to do it, and is going to do it with a vengeance in preference to allowing the Negro to have it. Now if the Negro cannot even get the farm hand's job, what is he going to get later on?"

Easter nodded in agreement, then together with dozens of others brought her hands together in applause. She turned her attention away from Marcus and scanned the crowd again; this time she spotted a tall man with skin the color of soot. Beside him stood a man of average size whose pallid complexion made him stand out like a lone star in a black sky.

"What has happened in this Missouri town is going to happen all over America, as seen through the vision and through the philosophy and through the teaching of the Universal Negro Improvement Association. I see that as clearly as I see you now. And that is why I have been giving my strength and my little intelligence to the program of the Universal Negro Improvement Association, because it will be a sad day when the Negro has nowhere to lay his head, and that day is coming—coming as sure as night follows day."

"He too black," Madeline announced when she caught Easter staring. "And besides," she added venomously, "he's a monkey chaser."

Easter jabbed Madeline in her side. She abhorred the names black Americans had for West Indians. It didn't matter what Madeline said, not a word had passed between Easter and the stranger and she was already intrigued. She stole another glance and then turned to Madeline. "How do you know that?"

Madeline's tone was condescending. "They look different from us. Like they just stepped out of the jungle. Can't you tell?"

"I think he's handsome."

"He would be if he wasn't so black."

"You ain't exactly light yourself, Mattie Mae Dawkins," Easter sneered.

The man saw Easter looking and smiled. Easter smiled back and he dropped his eyes, turned, and shared a few words with the man standing next to him. A few seconds later both men were walking toward her.

Madeline tugged the cuff of Easter's coat and hissed, "Let's go."

Easter deftly yanked her sleeve from Madeline's grip and turned to greet the tall, polished-looking man.

"Hello," he said. "My name is Colin and this is my friend Jack."

CHAPTER 11

The "getting to know you" part was easy. Coffee at a luncheonette accompanied by a shared slice of pie. Their forks became interlocked and they grinned sheepishly at each other over the calamity. A stroll through the park presented an opportunity for Colin to pluck a dandelion from its roots and fix it gently into her hair.

He slowly introduced her to his world, which was pinched into the tight corners of Harlem. In his world green bananas sunned on windowsills and cornmeal was turned with okra and dressed with a whole fish, whose dead eye glared accusingly up at Easter as she sunk her fork into the underside of its belly.

In his Harlem people sucked sugar straight from the cane, drank water from coconuts, mixed rice with peas, and doused everything with pepper sauce, even fried eggs. The people in his Harlem did not speak, they sang their way through conversations and disagreements, and it was there where she first heard the words *Junkanoo* and *Jouve*, enjoyed the fleshy sweetness of a mango, and became drunk from one too many cups of rum punch.

The people in that part of Harlem preferred dominoes to dice and could not for the life of them understand why football was called football when the feet had virtually no contact with the ball. Men and women in the part of Harlem that Colin claimed as his own greeted each other after six with *Good night* instead of *Good evening* and expressed their anger, disgust, and irritation by sucking their teeth.

Their music did not rely on piano or guitar, but instead put its trust in empty oil drums, frying pans, the lids of trash cans, and dried, hollowed-out bamboo reeds. They danced as if possessed. Spineless and sinful, they moved like Mama Rain.

"What kind of dancing do you call that?" Easter asked one night, already excited.

"*Wutless*," Colin said, taking her by the hands and leading her onto the dance floor.

He schooled her body in the art of his dance, resting his large palms on her slim hips, guiding them gently into the musical surf. Over time her inhibitions took shelter in the corner of the room and Easter allowed the music to swallow her, and so she did not blush when he pulled her into him and she felt his hardness pressing against her belly.

And oh, joy to the world—he was a book lover! Who had worn and well-read copies of *War of the Worlds*, *Dracula*, and *The Strange Case of Dr. Jekyll and Mr. Hyde*.

The two of them spent hours trolling through the stacks of books at the Aguilar Free Library on 110th and Third. Colin preferred hair-raising stories, while Easter fancied works that spoke less to the fantastic and more to the familiar—*Uncle Tom's Cabin* and *The Scarlet Letter*.

They'd take their books to Central Park, spread a blanket, and read to one another until the light vanished from the sky. Then they would go to his place—a tiny room located over a luncheonette. The air was always stale with the scents of grilled cheese and bitter coffee. It contained just two pieces of furniture—a bed and a stool. He kept his undergarments and socks draped over a hanger in the closet alongside his shirts and trousers.

When they made love the springs squealed loudly beneath the thin, hard mattress and they couldn't help but laugh. Afterwards they would whisper their pasts into each other's ears, and Colin cried when she told him about Rlizbeth. His tears touched her deep down in the soft, pink center of her soul.

Over time his name became a lump of sugar on her tongue that rolled off like syrup when she called out to him. When they were apart, he marched all through her mind and she found herself doing childish things like scrawling *Colin and Easter 4EVER* in the margins of her notebooks. Mattie Mae–now-Madeline almost died from laughter when she walked in on Easter posing in front of the mirror with the bed pillow stuffed beneath her dress.

"What you doing, girl?"

"Nothing," Easter responded in a huff, quickly tossing the pillow aside. She had woken up that morning a heartbeat away from hungover—she was so drunk with love for Colin. Later that same day she did something she never thought she'd ever do: she asked Colin for his hand in marriage.

"If you say no, I might have to kill myself," she joked, but there was a grave seriousness beneath the laughter. Colin was surprised and flustered and looked around for someone to tell him what to do or say, but it was just the two of them in his room. The sound of his beating heart filled the tiny space with the ferocity of a hundred drums.

He returned his gaze to Easter's waiting eyes and said the only thing that had come to mind: "Yes."

They were married on a Sunday in the parlor of number 17. Easter wore a cream dress with tiny blue silk flowers around the neckline and Colin, a gray sack coat, which he paired with black trousers because the moths had eaten holes in the gray ones.

CHAPTER 12

The store owners spotted spring's flouncing, flowered skirt way off in the distance and in preparation for her arrival sent their boys out with bucket and brush to scrub the pavement clean. Massive pots of lavender were set to boil and then poured out into the street to wash away the stench of stool and piss left behind by the police horses and stray canines. The fruit and vegetable vendors added a little extra shine to their apples and stacked them pyramid-style. Work rags popped and snapped against leather in a way they hadn't all winter long, and the shoeblacks sang in that ancient, mysterious way.

On the street those little boys whose first steps were a ball tap or step-heel tap were expert hoofers by the time they reached the age of five and they could roll, cramp, and Broadway shuffle with the best of them. Their jaw-dropping finales were aided by the fatback grease they slathered onto their knees, which allowed them to glide effortlessly across the cobblestone streets, hands thrust high above their heads and fingers fanned out like plumes.

If Easter could have planned it, she wouldn't have picked that day or that place. She had been on her feet for hours and reeked of pomade and fried hair. The day had warmed enough to leave the door open, allowing the sounds of the clanging bells of the trolleys that traveled along Lenox Avenue to seep into the shop and entwine with the women's incessant chatter.

Madeline was out front puffing on a cigarette and lollygagging with that broad-necked piano player called Fats Waller who played Chappo's monthly rent parties and had taken a liking to Madeline. Now he made it his business to come around a few times a week to slip a five-spot under her bra strap. Easter had asked her how many five-spots she thought he would give her before he demanded something in return. And Mattie Mae–now-Madeline had blinked stupidly at the question as if she didn't know that men always expected something in return—even if they hadn't given you a damn thing.

Mattie Mae–now-Madeline was playing with fire; it seemed that everyone except her knew that a season earlier, the boss's sister, Lumpkin Banks, had dropped her drawers for the musician, who had taken his fill and never returned, but left his specter behind to keep her warm for him, because sleep or wake Lumpkin could still feel him lying on top of her.

On that day that Easter would not have picked, and in that place she would not have chosen, Lumpkin stood in the doorway glaring at Mattie Mae and Fats Waller and so was completely oblivious to the woman waiting for her attention.

Sleek and luminous, the woman had caused a ruckus for three blocks prior to her arrival and two of the men who'd been especially struck by her good looks had followed her all the way to the threshold of the shop. Inside a hush settled over the women who were at various stages of beautification. Her arrival turned their expressions curious, then smug.

Who the hell does she think she is looking like that, dressing like that, with that good hair? Is she here to mock us?

One by one they reached up and shamefully touched the rough hair at the base of their necks and urged their hairdressers to get on with the slaying of the incorrigible curls.

"You Bibb?" the sleek woman asked for the second time.

Lumpkin responded without eye contact, "No, I'm Bibb's sister."

The woman waited a moment, sighed, looked down at her cuticles, and then said, "Need my hair done, I hear this is the place."

"Sink closest to the back wall."

Dark eyes followed the woman as she sashayed past them. Someone made a slanderous comment about the silk wrapped around her neck, but no one dared laugh. Easter was busy screwing a lid onto a jar when she happened to look up. Surely she was seeing an illusion. Rain was walking toward her, moving like an apparition through the rippling drapes of steam that rose from heads of hair being hot-combed into submission.

Easter couldn't believe her eyes, and she brought the back of her hand to her forehead to check for fever. It couldn't be her, Easter reasoned. She would have known Rain was in town. The earth would have moved, buildings would have crumbled—

"R-Rain?"

Rain gave her a flat look.

Had her appearance changed that much? Easter

quickly wiped the oil and perspiration from her face and snatched the hair cap from her head.

A spark flashed in Rain's eyes and then she offered a slight smile. "Easter?"

Throw yourself at me, girl, wrap those arms around me, kiss me full on the lips—I don't care who sees!

But that didn't happen. In the time they had been apart, it seemed that Rain had turned prim. Her lips curled and she said, "Imagine running into you here in Harlem."

Rain said this as if Harlem was the last place Easter should have been. Easter's jaw went slack and the women gazed indifferently at one another.

"You going to wash me or what?"

The matter-of-fact air of the statement struck Easter across her face. The flashback that followed caught her off guard—Rain's lips pressed against the lips of the girl—the memory lit a fire around her heart, and she saw herself lunging forward, catching Rain by her throat, and squeezing until her green eyes went dead.

"Easy now," Rain grinned and raised a cautious hand. "Can't you take a joke?"

Easter was still glaring at her.

"Girl, you look mad enough to kill!" Rain slapped her thigh and laughed.

Easter's face crumbled—a joke?—

"Serves you right," Rain said, "you sneaking off in the middle of the night without even a 'Goodbye, dog.'"

I would never call you a dog, not ever.

Rain took a step forward, her voice turned petal soft. "How do you think that made me feel?"

One tear, as big as a raindrop, dribbled from the corner of Easter's eye.

"Don't you start boo-hooing up in here, girl!" Rain's voice quivered with emotion. But it was already too late; both of their faces were wet when they finally embraced.

In the luncheonette the buzz of conversation competed with the sizzle of hamburgers and cheese sandwiches on the cook's grill. But Easter heard none of that and saw less. Her senses were devoted to Rain and Rain alone.

They'd taken a seat up front near the large window. "Tell me," Easter said, as the waitress set a cup of coffee down before her. She wanted to hear only those things that directly involved Rain. The minor characters were of no consequence to her. Rain could have simply fixed her green eyes on her and babbled *Me-me-me-me-me-me* for all eternity and Easter would have died a happy death.

So she began, her eyes swinging between Easter's intent gaze and the ceaseless stream of people that moved up and down the sidewalk.

Easter barely heard the story about the mob of white men with bad teeth and crazed eyes, wielding bats and shotguns, which raided Slocum's camp.

"Got the whole till." Rain shook her head. "Broke Slocum's arm and sliced the tip of his ear off."

Rain took a sip of her coffee and swirled the hot liquid around in her mouth. When she reached for her cigarette, Easter saw that her hand was shaking.

"That was it for me." Rain's voice seemed to come from a great distance. She leaned back into the pillowed leather backing of the booth, turned her head, and blew a thin stream of smoke into the aproned hip of a passing waitress. "They smacked me around some," she said, her eyes finding Easter's again. "Coulda been worse I guess. Coulda been dead, 'stead of sitting here talking to you." She fiddled with the knot in the silk scarf she wore around her neck.

Rain dead? Easter couldn't bear the thought of it.

"I left, went to Philly. Got some people there, you know . . ." She trailed off, snubbed the cigarette out, and quickly lit another one. She took a puff, licked her lips, and Easter almost died.

"Pie?"

"Here," Easter said irritably and pointed to the empty space on the table before dismissing the waitress with a sweep of her hand.

The waitress gave Easter a cruel look and walked away, grumbling to herself.

"You were saying." Easter used her fork to scoop up a large portion of pie.

Rain smoked and talked. There was a stop back home in New Orleans, a horrible fight with her sister, and an accusation made by a neighbor that cast Rain in a very bad light with the married women in her town.

"You know I don't care none about no niggers, Easter, you know niggers ain't got nothing to offer but a swinging dick!"

The last part was said in chorus; Easter, familiar with the bawdy phrase, had happily chimed in and they broke down with laughter until tears clung to their eyelashes.

A stint in Houston followed. "Crackers worse there than anywhere I ever been!"

Easter laughed so hard that water ran from her nose.

"I hightailed it back to New Orleans, stayed with an

uncle and his family. While I was there, my uncle told me that my son was living over in Covington."

She said "son" with a softness Easter didn't think Rain capable of.

"I ain't seen that boy since he was a tot," Rain spoke slowly. "Well you know, I told you all about that."

Easter nodded her head.

"My uncle said it was only right that I go see the boy. Said children need to look on their parents even if they don't know they're parents. He said the boy will have a better footing in the world. Good luck and all." She sighed and waved her hand. "Just some ole backwoods hoo-doo stuff.

"So me and my uncle go to Covington and can't for the life of us find the house. And we stop some folks and they say we not too far off, just down the road from where we headed. We get there and it's this shabby blue house with lace curtains in the window and a picket fence.

"I always wanted a house with a picket fence . . . Anyway, we walked up to the door and knocked and my stomach started to flutter cause I didn't know what I was gonna say to my child—my very own child—or what I was gonna do. I felt faint, Easter, I thought I was gonna drop down right there on that porch!"

Rain reached across the table and squeezed Easter's hands.

"The woman of the house opened the door and she wasn't the wife I remembered. She smiled and said hello and my Uncle Cleavus—did I tell you his name was Cleavus? Well, Cleavus took off his hat and asked if Charlie Youngblood lived there and the woman said, 'Yeah he live here, he my husband.'

"She looked us up and down and I guess we seemed harmless so she invited us on in. And then Cleavus pointed at me and said, 'This is my niece, Beulah—'"

Easter's jaw dropped and she coughed in surprise, "Beulah?"

Rain's eyes narrowed and she wagged her index finger in Easter's face. "And if you ever call me that I'll cut you," she hissed. "Anyway, we walked in and there was old Charlie, sitting in the parlor in his slacks and suspenders, no undershirt, mind you, and his gut was as big and as round as I don't know what! I look on him and saw that he wasn't even a shadow of what I'd known him to be.

"Charlie smiled when he saw my uncle and jumped up and said, 'Cleavus, you old dog you! What's it been, ten, twelve years? What you doing here in Covington?'

"They hugged and slapped one another on the backs and then Charlie looked over at me, and I could tell he didn't know me from a hole in the wall. But the wife got to looking at me hard and then something clicked in her head and her expression curdled just like sour milk.

"I stepped a little closer to Charlie, smiled real sweet, and said, 'Charlie, I'm hurt, you don't remember me.' He looked like he was staring down the throat of the devil and stepped back so quickly he knocked up against the china cabinet and sent all those ceramic figurines to rattling. The wife was by his side lickety-split, fussing over him and hollering *Baby this* and *Baby that*." Rain laughed. "He said, 'Sure I remember you, Beulah.' He looked at his wife and lied, 'I ain't seen her since she was a little itty-bitty thing,' and my uncle Cleavus nodded and went along with the lie.

"Then we all just stood there quiet and since no one seemed like they were gonna mention it, I said: 'So how your kids doing?' And the wife hopped straight up like something had bit her on the bottom of her feet."

Easter rubbed her hands together.

"Charlie grunted and said that the kids were fine, just fine. He say, 'Vaughn, my youngest boy, he helping me around the place, but he talking about following his brother, joining the army to serve his country. And me and my wife here, Lizzie, we got us a little girl name Corrine, she six years old.'"

Rain wiped at her mouth and then looked down at her hands. When she looked up again her eyes were wet and she had a dreamy look on her face. "My son's name is Vaughn . . . Right then their front door swung open and he walked in. I swear, Easter, I heard trumpets. Trumpets!"

Rain smacked the table with her hand.

"It wasn't no mistakin' that he was mine, ya hear me? That boy look like I spit him out. He look just like ME!" She wiped at her eyes and lit another cigarette. "Do you think every mother hears trumpets when their babies are around?" Her eyes blinked wildly, but Easter could tell from her tone that she was serious.

"I dunno, Rain, maybe."

"Well, I heard them as sure as I am a child of God, I heard trumpets! That boy of mine is so handsome. So tall and so handsome!" Her voice was filled with music. "Lord," she breathed. "Charlie, the old snake, told my boy that we were some folk he knew from back home. Had my child calling me Miss Beulah!"

Rain clapped her hands together and swayed to music only she could hear.

"I just couldn't stop staring at him and all I wanted to do was throw my arms around him."

Easter used the pad of her index finger to trace figure eights on the table. "So why didn't you?"

Rain's response was somber. "Cause if I had, I never would have let him go."

Rain used the napkin to dab at the corners of her eyes, and then retrieved her compact and lipstick from her purse. When she was done retouching her face she closed the compact with a sharp snap and Easter saw that only a residue of the softness remained.

"Well, ain't no use in crying over spilled milk, right? I went on to Gary, Indiana," Rain continued, "and after a week or so I fell ill." She shook her head in wonder. "It was like something had jumped on me and wouldn't turn loose. I thought I was going to check out of this life for sure."

Easter gulped.

"I sent a telegram to my friend Merry and she sent for me and I been here ever since."

"Who's Merry? How long you been here?" Easter didn't know which question she needed answered first.

"Oh," Rain turned her eyes up to the ceiling, "I been here 'bout six weeks now." She leaned back, brought her hand to her mouth, and used the nail of her pinky finger to dislodge something from between her teeth. "Merry is my good friend. My good, good friend," she proclaimed enthusiastically.

Easter's stomach knotted. "She the one from the tent?"

Rain looked confused. "What?"

"Nothing," Easter mumbled.

"Merry had her white doctor come up and check on me. He give me some tablets and in a few days I was feeling like my old self again."

"Her white doctor? Is *she* white?"

"Yes," Rain said pointedly.

Easter didn't want to hear anymore about this *good, good* friend and hastily changed the subject. "How did you know I was here?"

Rain smiled wryly. "I seen you with your Jody. I was in the car with Merry, she drive like a fool—I called out to you, but who could hear with all the ruckus on Lenox Avenue. I watched y'all kiss goodbye, then he went his way and you stepped into the shop. What's his name?"

Easter went blank for a minute. In that short time Colin had become a distant memory; even their morning frolic had slipped into oblivion. Up until the time Rain had appeared, she could still feel the impressions of his fingers on her backside. But now . . . it was like he'd never been born. Easter felt ashamed, as if marrying Colin had somehow sullied her love for Rain.

She wanted to ask, *Do you forgive me?* But instead, she grimaced and announced, "We're married."

Rain's eyes bulged and her face broke into a huge smile. She reached over and playfully slapped the back of Easter's hand.

"Sure nuff?"

Easter nodded.

"Well, congratulations!" she wailed, clapping her hands together.

Easter reached for her spoon, muttered a barely audible "Thank you," and then dunked the utensil into the cold cup of coffee.

Rain waited. She expected something more than a thank you. A story perhaps—one that chronicled their meeting, courtship, and nuptials—but Easter remained mute, her gaze fixed on the dark, swirling funnel her stirring spoon conjured in the cold cup of joe.

"So y'all got any babies?"

Easter shook her head. She'd stopped using the vinegar pouch and still her menstrual arrived every month like clockwork. Colin wasn't worried; he said God would know when the time was right. But Easter was concerned and wondered if during the abortion Chappo had removed something from her that she shouldn't have.

"Well I—I hope I get to meet this husband of yours."

Easter shrugged her shoulders, but kept her eyes lowered.

Rain smoothed her hair, which signified yet another shift in the conversation. "So," she leaned in and asked, "you still writing those stories?"

Was she still writing those stories? That was like asking a former slave if he still wanted to be free. Of course she was still writing those stories. Writing kept her sane, kept her from spinning out of control, kept her tongue still whenever some white person spoke down to her. She *had* to write, it was the only thing that was completely hers, that she could look forward to at the end of her long day. There wasn't one thing she owned that hadn't belonged to someone before her, not a thread of clothing or pair of shoes—even the bed she and her husband slept on and their tattered sofa had had previous owners. But her stories didn't belong to anyone else. She couldn't even say that about the silver wedding band that graced her finger.

You goddamn right she was still writing, writing like a fiend sometimes, writing herself into a fervor that left her shaken and drenched, writing until her fingers cramped and her spine ached, writing straight through the night and into the blue day.

Was she still writing? She was writing to keep a grip on life, the evidence of which was right there on the skin of her index and middle fingers—dark indentations from the pencils she used. Was she still writing? Well, she had to leave something of herself behind, something that said she'd been there and had made a contribution, because she sensed that her body would never yield a child. So her stories had become her babies. And the fact that her babies were conceived in her mind and not her womb did not make them any less alive, any less beautiful, any less loved, or any less glorious.

"Yeah, I'm still writing," she said.

CHAPTER 13

Colin cocked his head and listened to the silence and wondered why it was he couldn't hear the sound of his life crumbling away. The signs had been there for some time. Those dreams of him waking to find that he'd lost every tooth in his mouth. And what of the one of him flying through the sky as natural as a swallow? And the nightmare that brought him the most uneasiness, the one where he climbed from his bed, walked to the window, and looked out to find that Harlem was gone, replaced with the turquoise sea of his homeland. The water was dotted with brightly painted wooden boats, holding erect fishermen, their muscled arms flexing as they cast their nets out over the waters. Sea gulls swooped and screamed in the sky above their heads, and on the sandy shore stood his mother, starfish and sea eggs scattered at her feet, hands cupped around her mouth as she shouted his name across the placid blue. From his window Colin waved to his mother and called, "I'm here, Mum, I'm here!" And that's when the sea began to ripple and the boats bounced. The sky grew dark and in the distance the sea roared, arched its wet back, and came crashing to shore. When the waters receded, the sea gulls were gone, the fishermen and their boats were gone, and so was his mother.

He always woke from that dream shaken, drenched

in perspiration with the smell of sea water in his nostrils. And now, as he sat on the stoop solemnly smoking a cigarette, he realized that the dream had finally come to fruition, the evidence of which was clutched tightly in his hand.

The letter was from his Aunt Nita but written in the hand of a neighbor. It said that his mother was sick, the roof of the house was falling in, the shop's shelves were empty and thus its doors were closed and locked, and the pigs were dying of a mysterious disease. He was needed back home and if he couldn't come, he needed to send money.

Colin was in no position to do either. Over the past year he and Easter had managed to save one hundred and seventy five dollars, all of which he used to purchase—without Easter's consent or knowledge—thirty-five shares of Marcus Garvey's Black Star Line stock. According to what he'd been reading in the newspapers, the stock was now worth shit.

Colin reached up, dug his fingers into his wooly hair, and gave his scalp a good scratching; the action normally helped to clear his mind, but on that day his thoughts were like bricks and the weight was bringing on a migraine.

And then there was that woman, his wife's friend. He'd met her just twice. The first time Easter came blustering into the apartment, Rain behind her, they were giggling like schoolgirls. Colin was down the hall in the bathroom, heard Easter's jubilant laughter echoed by that of a stranger. As he reached for the doorknob, he heard the stranger say, "You remember how to do it, girl? Lemme see."

When he walked into the room, Easter's back was to

him and she had her skirt hiked up so high he could see her bloomers. Her legs were flapping like wings. Rain looked up at him and smiled. "Well, hello."

Easter swung around and the hem of the skirt fell from her hands. "Hi," she stammered, her tone filled with disappointment. She said nothing else.

Colin looked at Rain, extended his hand, and said "Hello, I'm Colin Gibbs, Easter's husband."

She took his hand in hers and said simply, "Rain."

"Oh, I don't know where my mind is." Easter brushed at her skirt and asked, "Baby, what are you doing home?"

"It's my day off," Colin reminded her without pulling his eyes from Rain's smiling face. "Rain? Oh yes, Easter has spoken of you. So nice to finally meet you."

Her hand was warm, her grip strong.

"Same here."

"Can I get you something to drink? A Coca-Cola?"

"Sure, thanks." Rain crossed her legs.

Easter stood stupidly by, not knowing what to do or say. Colin gave her a passing glance as he used his teeth to pry the cap from the bottle and then handed it to Rain.

"Are you visiting?"

Rain huffed, "Something like that."

Colin watched as Rain tilted the bottle to her mouth and drank. She wore a black scarf wound loosely around her neck, and he was sorry for the obstruction, for some reason he wanted to see her throat.

"Oh?" Colin sat down in the chair opposite the sofa. "Easter didn't say you were coming to town."

"She didn't know."

"She saw me . . . *us* on the street last week," Easter

spouted as she moved to the sofa and sank down beside Rain. "She didn't even know I was living in Harlem."

Colin ignored her. "Where are you staying?"

"With a friend on Edgecombe Avenue."

"Sugar Hill?" Colin made a face. He didn't know of any Negroes living up there. "*Fan-cy*," he added.

"Her friend is a writer," Easter spoke rapidly. "Rain is going to show her some of my stories."

Colin looked at Easter. "For what?"

"To see if maybe she can get them published," Rain said, and set the empty bottle down onto the table.

A look of surprise passed across Colin's face. This was news to him. Easter had never mentioned a word about publishing her stories. As far as he was concerned it was a pastime, like knitting or needlepoint. He looked at his wife and she avoided his gaze.

Colin shook these thoughts from his head. He had to stay focused on what needed to be done in the here and now. He rose, straightened his pant legs, and headed toward the UNIA headquarters on 135th Street. He'd speak with Marcus Garvey personally; he'd explain his situation. Garvey was an intelligent man; he knew the hardships his brethren faced. He'd give him his money back, Colin was sure of it.

CHAPTER 14

Number 409 Edgecombe Avenue sat south of 155th Street. The building had been designed by Schwartz and Gross and climbed thirteen stories into the sky. The imposing red-brown brick structure was one of the most desirable addresses in the Sugar Hill section of Harlem. The only colored people who came and went from 409 were nannies, cooks, butlers, maids, and lift operators.

After a thorough tour of the penthouse, which was so massive that it enclosed twenty-one servants' rooms, Meredith Tomas had paid a year's worth of rent, signed the lease, and pocketed the keys.

"I'm sure you and Mr. Tomas will be very happy here," Art Ball, the superintendent, had announced with feigned sincerity. As far as he was concerned the climate in Harlem was changing for the worse. South of 155th Street had been infested with coons and monkeys who were gradually swarming north and no doubt one day soon would invade his beloved 409, bringing with them their stench and jungle bunny ways, and he would have no choice but to leave, because nothing could make him answer to a nigger, no less an entire apartment building filled with them.

He'd already begun making inquiries about positions on the elegant and staunchly white Lower East Side.

And so it was no surprise to Art Ball when on that blustery October morning his prediction became horribly true and Meredith MacDougal Tomas walked into 409 Edgecombe linked arm in arm with her bronze-colored Cuban husband, Eduardo.

Meredith Tomas, the only child of Tabitha and Conrad MacDougal, was born and raised in Michigan. Her father had made his fortune in real estate. The family lived in a sprawling mansion on Iroquois in Detroit's Indian Village. Edsel Ford, son of the auto baron Henry Ford, lived just two houses away with his wife Eleanor and their children.

Meredith attributed her love of everything African to Edsel, who traveled to the continent several times and became an enthusiastic collector of its artifacts.

"Something stirred in me the first time Edsel let me hold a Senegalese fertility mask," Meredith would purr whenever she told the story. "And I've been smitten ever since."

Meredith met her husband Eduardo at a cocktail party at the exclusive Grosse Pointe Yacht Club. She'd mistaken the tall, dark, and excruciatingly handsome third-generation tobacco plantation owner for a waiter, since the yacht club was exclusionary, so the only people of color allowed inside were the help.

Allowances had been made for Eduardo Tomas to gain entrance, as he was a guest of Oren Scotten of the Scotten-Dillon Tobacco Company. Oren had been courting Eduardo and his acres of Cuban tobacco gold for some time.

Scotten needed the yacht club to solidify the deal, because every deal he'd ever closed inside those white walls had gone on to be profitable beyond his expectations. He was a superstitious man and he wasn't about to jinx his streak of good luck just because some blue-blood socialites couldn't break bread with an *Oyé*.

Eduardo signed the contract and extended his trip, to make time to court the beautiful Meredith MacDougal. A scandalous affair had ensued. Meredith was a brazen lover, willing to do anything to please him sexually, and Eduardo found himself exthralled in a way he had never been with Maria, his wife of fifteen years.

His mind made up, Eduardo took Meredith's hand in his and asked her to be his wife.

To Meredith, Eduardo represented the ultimate accessory, the consummate conversation piece: tall, handsome, and exotic. She would be the first one in her circle to defy convention. Meredith tousled Eduardo's hair and said yes.

A speedy divorce followed and Eduardo evicted his wife and three children from his palatial Havana estate, relocating them to a modest second home in Las Tunas. Three months later Eduardo married Meredith in a lavish ceremony at the Hotel Plaza in Havana. The wedding made the front page of *El Diario de la Marina*, relegating the death of Grace McLaughlin, the missing American heiress who had eloped with her married lover to Cuba four months earlier, to the lower left-hand corner of page eight.

CHAPTER 15

Easter and Colin stared at the cucumber sandwiches that the servant had set down before them and Easter wondered if white people truly enjoyed that type of food or if it was all for show and when out of the sights of colored folk, they hungrily gorged themselves on pig's feet and Johnny cake.

"I really loved your work," Meredith leaned forward and said. "It resonated with me in a way that I never thought it would." She reached her hand out for one of the sandwiches and then decided against it. "I can't believe you're not published."

Easter tried to focus on Meredith's gray eyes, and on the words that were streaming from between her thin lips, but she was distracted by the strands of pearls that hung in waves around her neck and the precious baubles that graced her fingers, and how Rain was sitting so close to Meredith their hips touched.

Colin was fidgeting.

He was a simple man and was uncomfortable with the lavish surroundings. He felt intimidated by the crystal chandelier and offended by the expensive oil paintings that hung on the walls. He found it hard to meet the eyes of the black female servant who brought him his drink, as if his being a guest of the white aristocrat was somehow a slight against her, against their race.

And that woman. That Rain. She was fooling herself if she thought her light skin and green eyes made her one of *them*. Hadn't she heard of the one-drop rule?

"You have a phenomenal voice and I think with some polishing . . ."

Colin pulled at his tie; the knot was cutting off his air supply and he'd begun to perspire. When Meredith interrupted her monologue to ask if he would like another drink, he said yes too quickly.

"Polishing? But I thought you said they were good." Easter sounded wounded.

"Oh they are, darling, they are, but . . ."

Colin raised the glass and drank.

He hated them, these white people who had everything. He looked over at Easter and began to scrutinize her. The dress she wore was old and the color faded. She wore dull hair pulled back into a ball. Her shoes were scuffed and the heels worn down to the nail.

The servant brought him another drink without Meredith having to tell her. The liquor made Colin feel confident and he finally found the nerve to look up and into the servant's eyes. There was nothing there, save for complacency. She was a trained seal. They all were. Including him.

Colin shifted on the sofa, working hard to contain the anger that was bubbling in his stomach. He swallowed the liquor and the servant brought him another.

"They're good, but they're raw. And raw is not a bad thing. I just think with some tutelage they could be better."

His mother was sick, her house was falling apart, the shop was closed and his pigs were dying, and this woman was talking about *tutelage*? Everything he had worked hard for was going to rot and she was talking about tutelage. He needed some tutelage right about now, preferably in the form of a check.

Money.

He'd borrowed five dollars from his friend Jack and sent it off to his mother with the promise of more to come. That was two weeks ago and he hadn't heard anything back yet. He'd gone to the UNIA headquarters on three separate occasions to speak with Marcus Garvey in person and each time was told that Marcus was traveling. Jack, an officer with the UNIA, had confirmed this and then asked if there was anything he could help him with. Colin had said no, and then yes, and Jack ended up lending him the money.

"I can help you. I mean, if you want my help, that is," Meredith said to Easter.

Colin's eyes roamed the room and lit on a set of silver candlesticks. He thought he could live for a year on what those candlesticks would bring him. They were just sitting there looking pretty; she probably never even used them. Rich people did things like that. They spent extraordinary amounts of money on things that looked pretty but served no real purpose. They bought expensive clothes for specific occasions and then never wore them again. They purchased cars that they never drove, preferring instead to stash them away in warehouses. They bought wine they didn't drink, jewelry they rarely wore, and vast estates they only visited once a year. In Colin's opinion, they were an excessive, wasteful people.

"You could help me with my work. I write in longhand as well and my secretary usually transcribes—"

"Transcribes?"

"Yes, she transcribes my written notes to typeface. Can you type?"

No she couldn't, though she had seen it done. It looked simple enough. How hard could it be?

"Yes."

Colin was drunk and could barely stand up when it came time for them to leave. The butler brought him his hat and it slipped from Colin's hands and fell to the floor. The butler made no move to retrieve it and Colin was in no condition to make the attempt, so Easter stooped down and picked it up.

On the street Colin tripped over his feet and swayed drunkenly from side to side. In the streetcar, he plopped heavily down into a seat and began talking loudly.

The closer they got to their neighborhood, the more contentious and hostile his babbling became. Easter remained stone-faced and silent. There was no use trying to speak to him while he was in that state. And she realized as they climbed off the trolley and started up the street that he was in that state more and more frequently.

When she'd first met Colin, he had not been a drinking man, but that had changed. Whatever life circumstance had triggered that change he wasn't saying, and Easter was tired of asking.

CHAPTER 16

Jack Jones turned the desk lamp off, rose from his chair, gathered the receipts, stacked them neatly, placed them in the bottom drawer of his desk, and locked it. He pulled the shades down over the windows before walking out of the office and down the steps to the lower level of the brownstone that housed the UNIA headquarters.

The kitchen was thick with the scent of herring and boiled yams. Sitting at the square table were three men of various shapes and sizes. "Rum?" one of the men suggested, nodding at the bottle in the center of the table. Jack shook his head as he reached for a chair.

"You eat?" another asked.

Jack raised his hand and said, "I'm good."

Wesley Payne, one of Marcus Garvey's generals, reached for the bottle and poured until the amber liquor reached the rim of the glass. He drank deeply and made a face as the liquor burned a fiery trail down his throat. He gasped, slapped his chest, and asked Jack, "How many today?"

"Two hundred thirty-five."

A murmur of satisfaction passed around the table. Wesley grinned. "That's nearly a thousand shares of stock sold this week alone."

"When will Marcus be back?" Jack asked casually.

"The end of the week."

Jack nodded, stood, and bid the men goodnight. He took the train down to Greenwich Village. On the street he was vaguely aware of the crunching sound his shoes made against the frozen snow. The sky above his head was dark, the moon and its cousins hid behind clouds that threatened more snow.

Jack headed to Chumley's, which was located at 86 Bedford Street. He stepped in and allowed the door to close nosily behind him. He stood in the vestibule stomping the packed snow from his shoes and then shrugged off his coat and stepped into the warm, dimly lit bar.

The embers in the fireplace glowed and crackled as Jack moved past men and women seated at booths and round tables, embroiled in conversation. He slid into a booth located in the rear, where the shadows were thickest.

"What can I get fer ya?" the brawly waiter with shockingly blue eyes asked.

"Coffee."

The history of Chumley's made him uneasy. Why they'd chosen that particular place to meet was not entirely beyond him. Chumley's had been a refuge for runaway slaves. He imagined that the meeting place made great fodder for jokes amongst his colleagues.

A few minutes later two white men joined him. Even though Jack Jones had the color and features of an Anglo, he felt conspicuous sitting between the two men. In a line-up he was sure one of his own could confidently pick him out as a spade masquerading as an ofay.

"How many today?" the larger of the two men asked.

"Two hundred thirty-five," Jack responded.

The smaller man let off a long whistle. "That nigger—no offense, Jack—is really pulling in the cash, ain't he?"

Jack said, "None taken," but his jaw was clenched. "And he's in negotiations to purchase another vessel."

The two men exchanged looks of surprise. The smaller man laughed, "I've got to give it to him, he's got heart."

"That he has," said the other man.

"Imagine, he wants to take Negroes back to Africa. Africa, for God's sake! We get 'em here and get 'em halfway civilized and they wanna go back to Africa and live like savages again."

Now both men laughed. Jack raised his cup to his lips and drank. The smaller one reached for his hat and set it firmly onto his head. Still laughing, he asked the larger man, "What is that catch phrase he's using to rile up the Negroes?"

The larger man rolled his eyes in thought and tapped at his chin. "I can't remember."

"Africa for Africans," Jack said in a low voice, and raised the cup to his lips again.

"Yeah, that's it!" the two white men cried in unison.

Who are you? the voice echoed in Jack's head as he rode the train back uptown. The voice always came after he left Chumley's. He wasn't a superstitious man; he didn't believe in ghosts, haints, or juju. Besides, he knew it was none of those things; the voice in his head was clearly his own.

As he trudged home, the snow finally began to fall, sugaring his hat and the top of his coat. At that late hour he had Harlem to himself. Jack stopped walking, tilted his head back, and opened his mouth. The flakes melted instantly on his warm tongue.

He remained that way for some time, his mind drifting back to his childhood in Massachusetts when he and his family lived in a community of Octoroons. Did they think themselves better than other Negroes? Maybe not always better than—but certainly better off. They could move among the whites unnoticed, gaining access to places their darker cousins would never be welcomed. The idea of living that way forever was seductive, and many fell under the spell and made the small leap from black to white, often never to be heard from again. But living a duplicitous life was a curse and a blessing. Jack had witnessed several young women who passed to marry white men. A year or so later they would return to the community, shame-faced and distraught, cradling mocha-colored newborns.

One drop.

Jack climbed the stairs of 28 West 133rd Street and inserted his key into the lock. He walked into his small room and removed his hat and coat.

The voice sounded again: *Who are you?*

Jack ignored it and moved to the vent to warm his frozen hands.

Every day he gathered information on Marcus Garvey and the activities of the UNIA. The U.S. government had labeled Garvey an anarchist. He was to Negroes what Emma Goldman was to women. Dangerous Emma had called for access to birth control—how dare she suggest a woman be in control of her own reproductive system!

And so, too, how dare Marcus Garvey suggest that Negroes develop and maintain their own economic system? How dare he put it into their minds that they could return to Africa, form their own government in Liberia, and unite the continent as one massive, indestructible force?

Africa for Africans!

Marcus Garvey's words rang in Jack's head. He moved across the room to the small looking glass that hung on the closet door and gazed wondrously at the man in the mirror. His mind shouted out: *Who are you?*

He was a black man encased in white skin who faithfully served a hypocritical government, which had expressed, through a variety of laws and lack thereof, its blatant loathing and disregard for its Negro populace, and had the audacity to become outraged when those same Negroes sought to pack up and leave these United States.

Africa for Africans!

Why couldn't the government just let them go? Be rid of the lazy, nasty, stupid, murderous, thieving, raping, lying coons once and for all? Did white people need Negroes to make them feel good about themselves? To be their whipping boys, their entertainment? Certainly they could have one of their own scrub their floors, wash their clothes, and raise their children.

Why?

It always came down to that one word: why?

And when Jack arrived at that point—as he did every time he had this particular inward conversation—he found that he had no answer.

Who are you!

Jack finally responded: *I am James Wormley Jones, the first ever Negro FBI agent, assigned by Hoover himself. I am Special FBI agent 800, James Wormley Jones, assigned to infiltrate the UNIA organization and to report on all activities!*

The man in the mirror smirked. *But who are you* really?

James Wormley Jones opened his closet door and pulled from the shelf a shoe box containing his special agent FBI pistol. He closed the door and his reflection was still waiting for an answer.

He released the safety on the gun.

I am a rat-fink, sell-out . . .

He cocked the hammer and pressed the nozzle to his temple.

An Uncle Tom house nigger.

He squeezed his eyes shut and rested the pad of his index finger against the trigger and found, just as he had numerous times before, that he couldn't do it, because above all, he was weak.

CHAPTER 17

Eduardo Tomas gave his wife a sharp look. It had been months since her friend, the woman with the ridiculous name, had appeared on their doorstep. As far as he was concerned, Rain had well overstayed her visit, and had over-indulged in their food, liquor, and was taking advantage of Meredith's generosity. Didn't Meredith see that Rain was a leech? And now she was talking about taking Rain to Paris! It was more than Eduardo could bear and so he exploded.

"I won't have it!" he barked, and brought his fist down onto the breakfast table. The eggs, bacon, and toast trembled on their porcelain plates and the coffee swilled over the edge of the gold-embossed cup.

Meredith batted her eyes. "You won't have what, darling?"

And now there was another. A darker one with quiet ways who showed up every other evening and pecked mercilessly away on the typewriter until all hours of the night.

Who did Meredith say she was? Oh yes, her secretary.

What kind of spell did these *changos* have over his wife? She surrounded herself with them. She donated money to their useless causes, ladled soup in their poorhouses, cradled their babies in their orphanages, and now she had one living in their home.

"I won't allow you to squander any more of my money on that *puta*!"

She dressed like a *puta*, spoke like one, drank like one, and moved like one. And the places she spent her time, down there in Jungle Alley singing and baring her breasts—only *putas* did that.

She was a bad influence on his wife.

Meredith lowered the newspaper she'd been reading and looked at her husband with a knitted brow. "*Puta*? Really, darling, such language so early in the morning?"

Eduardo bristled. "I am not making fun with you, Merry. I mean it, no more!" His arm swept through the air and knocked over a crystal vase filled with geraniums. The butler appeared in a flash, cloth in hand, and began to attend to the mess.

Meredith stiffened.

"When I come back from Havana, I want her gone." He was absolute, and without another word he stormed from the room.

Rain never rose before noon. But that morning the commotion roused her and she removed the pink satin sleep mask from her eyes and peered into the milky darkness of her bedroom. Her head was heavy, her throat dry, and her feet swollen. The culprit was the excessive amount of gin she'd consumed before bed.

The front door slammed and the windows rattled. Outside her bedroom she could hear the *tap*, *tap*, *tap* of Bijou, the gray and white Malti-Poo, as he followed close on Meredith's heels. One knock and the door slowly opened. Meredith's distressed voice reached through the darkness. "Rain? Rain, darling, are you awake?"

Rain raised her hand and waved.

"No, Bijou, no," Meredith chastised as she used her slippered foot to gently nudge the dog back out into the hallway. "Darling," she breathed dramatically, rushing to the bed, "Eduardo is not at all happy with our little jaunt across the water. He is being a complete monster!"

Rain threw back the coverlet.

Meredith unknotted the belt of her silk robe, slipped her arms from the belled sleeves, and allowed the material to crumple to the floor. "You must see Paris—everyone must see Paris before they die!"

She was stark naked. Her small breasts curved upwards, the nipples were erect and pink. She climbed into the bed and wrapped her sinewy arms around Rain's neck.

"He spoke to me in the most horrendous manner," she said, bringing her face close to Rain's. "And he called you a *puta!*"

Rain kissed her, a deep, passionate kiss that sent a lightning bolt of excitement through both of their bodies.

"He wants you to go. He says you must be out by the time he returns." Meredith's voice was full of sadness. She pressed her palm against Rain's cheek. "I won't allow it, I won't," she sobbed.

Rain pulled Meredith to her and laid her head against her breasts. "Shhhh," Rain consoled as she lovingly stroked Meredith's hair. "Don't worry, I'm not going anywhere."

CHAPTER 18

When Colin first complained, Easter brushed it off, called him silly, wrapped her arms around his neck, and used baby talk to assure him that he had nothing to be concerned about. She told him that he was her big strong husband and all she and Rain were doing was getting reacquainted and reminiscing about old times.

Colin had acquiesced, but could not ignore the perpetual bliss that Easter had worn like a cloak ever since Rain stepped back into her life. She was positively buoyant; it was as if Easter was living on a great body of water. Colin half expected her to leave puddles of salty water in her wake. He'd never had that type of effect on her and he was her husband. His ego imploded.

The second time he broached the subject, Easter's response was cutting and she accused him of being childish and selfish and pointed out that she never uttered a word about all the time he spent down at the UNIA headquarters.

When she began working over at Meredith's apartment, he held his tongue. But what started out as one night a week had progressed into two and then three, and now she was spending her one day off over there with *them* instead of with him, her husband. And when she *was* home all she talked about was Rain and Meredith.

Colin looked at Easter, really looked at her, and for the first time he saw her naïveté. It was shining like a star right in the center of her forehead. How had he missed it all this time?

"I don't understand why you don't hate them."

They'd had this conversation a million times. And the thought of revisiting it yet again made Easter weary.

"They raped your sister. They lynched and burned your friend—you saw it with your own damn eyes!"

Easter sat down on the sofa, reached for one Colin's cigarettes, and lit it.

"What they do to your people here in this country is disgraceful, yet you run to the buckra in her fancy apartment in the sky and you lick her ass." His chest heaved and he bared his teeth like a wild animal.

Easter didn't know what language she needed to make him understand. Did she love white people? She would not go so far as to say that, but she couldn't say she hated them, not as a race. She tried to judge *all* people on an individual basis.

But Colin needed her to hate, he needed her to feel what he felt and know it. "Come with me," he said, and grabbed his hat.

She had never been to the Bronx, not once in the few years she'd been living in New York. He said they were going to the zoo, but his face was solemn and dark, an expression best suited for a visit to a funeral parlor or gravesite.

They boarded the train and Easter rested her head on the window and watched the scenery peel by. Her thoughts were not on their destination, but on Rain. She wondered what she was doing at that very moment.

Colin took her hand and practically dragged her through the arched gates of the zoo. They sped past the caged sea lions, the sleeping leopards, the yawning tigers, and the cages filled with chattering rainbow-colored birds, until they found themselves at the entrance to the monkey house. Easter opened her mouth, a question balanced on her tongue, but Colin raised a finger to her lips.

Once they were inside his grip tightened around her hand as he edged his way through the throng of fascinated onlookers. Easter could see bright orange fur and huge droopy eyes pressed into an elongated face. An orangutan? He brought her all this way to see an orangutan?

They moved closer until they were right up front and Easter found herself staring at a man, who gazed back at her from the opposite side of the metal bars. She thought her mind was playing a cruel trick on her eyes, but when she blinked he was still there. The orangutan threw his arms around the man's shoulders and hugged him. The man hugged him back and then shrugged him off.

The white people laughed, and some of them hunched their backs, pushed out their bottom lips, and made whooping monkey sounds.

Easter's eyes roamed to the sign posted on the enclosure:

The African Pygmy, "Ota Benga."
Age 28, Height 4 feet 11 inches.
Congo Free State, South Central Africa.
By Dr. Samuel P. Verner.

The natural emotion should have been anger and embarrassment, but all Easter wanted to do was cry. She looked up at her husband and her eyes asked what her mouth couldn't: *Why did you bring me here?*

Ota Benga was naked except for a loincloth. And as was the custom of his people, his teeth had been filed to sharp and precise points. In his hand he held a child's bow and arrow, which he trained first on the orangutan and then squarely on the crowd. Some of the male on-lookers clutched their chests and stumbled backwards on the heels of their expensive leather shoes, crying, "Ow, you got me!"

The ladies twirled their parasols and giggled behind hands encased in delicately embroidered gloves as they watched their children toss peanuts through the bars, even though there was a sign that read, *Please Do Not Feed the Animals.*

Ota Benga spotted Easter and Colin—the only two dark faces in the sea of white—and pleasure spread across his face in a smile. He rushed excitedly to the front of the cage, wrapped his fingers around the bars, and proudly announced: "I. Am. Man."

On the way back home, Colin was satisfied that he had accomplished what he'd set out to do. He didn't have to ask Easter if she finally felt the hate. He knew she did, he could see it oozing out of her like pus.

CHAPTER 19

That night Easter dreamed of blood. The next day she went to work and did not smile for the entire day. When Mattie Mae–now-Madeline asked what her problem was, Easter pressed her lips together and shrugged her shoulders. One woman after the next came to her sink and she scrubbed, rinsed, and massaged their scalps, but she did not make small talk and uttered a barely audible "Thank you" when they dropped the quarter tip into her open palm.

She could not erase Ota Benga from her mind. He was stuck there, nailed into her memory for all eternity—him and those three little words that crushed her heart.

And what had the white people done when he spoke those words? They laughed and clapped their hands and shouted, "Now say 'Polly wanna cracker'!"

The morning stretched into afternoon. The clock on the wall struck noon and with it came a squeal from one of the hairdressers. The entire shop shuddered and Easter looked up to see that Lumpkin had Mattie Mae–now-Madeline pinned against the paned glass wall of the shop. One hand was flat against Mattie Mae–now-Madeline's chest, while the other held tight to the wooden handle of a hot comb; its metal teeth glowed crimson and hovered just inches from her jugular.

She didn't utter a word, she didn't even breathe, as Lumpkin screamed into her face, "I told you he's mine!"

Without thinking, Easter snatched up a pair of barber's scissors from a nearby station. In a flash she was behind Lumpkin, the business end of her weapon pressed against Lumpkin's neck.

A collective gasp went up from the women in the shop.

"This don't have nothing to do with you, Easter," Lumpkin sneered.

Easter shifted her eyes to Mattie Mae–now–Madeline and smiled assuredly at her friend. "It's got everything to do with me, Lumpkin."

"Well, then I guess me and Madeline both going to meet our maker today."

Lumpkin moved the hot comb closer and Madeline's skin went tender and pink beneath the heat. Soon it would begin to blister. Easter applied pressure, piercing Lumpkin's flesh. A thin stream of red spilled from the puncture and pooled in the hollow curve of her collarbone.

Lumpkin's face contorted with pain. "Your friend? This roach ain't got a lick of respect for me. I done told her time and time again to leave be my man. But do she mind what I say? No! She throw herself at him every chance she get. She ain't nothing but a hussy, and I'm gonna take care of that, cause those who can't hear will feel!"

Lumpkin's face disintegrated right before Easter's eyes and was replaced with a collage of white faces belonging to people who had hurt her family and friends.

Blood flooded Easter's ears and she howled inwardly, and she almost did it, she almost stuck Lumpkin like a pig.

"Look here, Lumpkin, Mattie Mae is a fool for sure. You right, you done told her numerous times to leave be your man and she ain't mind. But her hard ears don't call for this. Mattie Mae is like family to me. We come from the same town, played in the same dirt, swam in the same lake. Her mama whipped my ass like I was her'n and my mama did the same to Mattie Mae. We got history, ya hear? So when you say I ain't got nothing to do it with it, you dead wrong. Me and Mattie Mae is wrapped up tight like a ball of string. So if you burn her, I swear 'fore God I will cut you."

Lumpkin swallowed hard and when she spoke again, most of the fight had left her voice. "You better tell her to mind then, Easter. She better mind what I say or next time . . ."

Easter nodded her head. "There won't be no next time," she said smoothly, her eyes fixed on Mattie Mae–now-Madeline, "will there?"

"N-no," Mattie Mae–now-Madeline stammered.

"You hear what Lumpkin say, right Madeline? Fats is her Jody not your'n."

Madeline slowly nodded her head.

Satisfied, Lumpkin lowered the hot comb; it slipped from her fingers and went clanging to the black-and-white tiled floor.

After that Easter wet a towel and told Mattie Mae–now-Madeline to hold it against her neck. She did the same for Lumpkin and then went to sit down for a spell. She looked around the place she had worked since she came up north and the shop suddenly seemed small and cramped and that familiar feeling began to creep through her.

It was time to move on.

Easter stood, removed her apron, rolled it into a ball, and dumped it into a hamper. She had her pocketbook slung over her shoulder and was halfway to the door when Mattie Mae–now-Madeline called out, "Where you going?"

"Home."

"You coming back?"

"No."

Minutes later, she was hit with the shakes so bad that she barely made it up the stairs and into bed.

When Colin finally came home, his eyes were blood-shot and watery. He found Easter buried under layers of blankets, shivering so badly he could hear her teeth chattering. He stumbled over to the bed and glowered down at her. "You sick?"

Easter opened her mouth to answer, but Colin cut her off and spat, "My mum is dead," and with that he tossed a crumpled ball of paper at her, staggered over to the table where Easter had laid her purse, snatched it up, turned it over, and dumped out the contents. The only money she had were the tips she'd made that morning—one dollar and fifty cents. He raked the bill and the coins into his hand and left.

Easter waited until she heard the front door close before she retrieved the ball of paper and unfurled it. The telegram read:

Colin Gibbs.
Marda Gibbs passed away yesterday at 3:15PM.
Send money for burial.
Your aunt Nita.

Easter looked at the door. Her heart pained for her husband. She knew what it was to lose a mother.

It was just after six in the evening, but a noonday sun was still beating down on New York City, raising the mercury to a sizzling ninety-eight degrees. Colin moved through the streets oblivious to the heat, in fact he walked as if in winter, with a bustling gait that caused people to pause and stare at him. So the next day when his picture graced the front page of the local newspapers, more than a few dozen mouths uttered: "I remember him; he did have the look of a man who could kill."

CHAPTER 20

B ack in the apartment, Easter reached for her Bible, the place where they kept their savings. Colin's mother was dead. Of course he would have to go home to Barbados and say his final goodbye.

Easter turned the book over, clutched it by the spine, and waved it briskly through the air. The pages flapped noisily, but not a dollar fell. The money was gone.

She rushed from the apartment and ran all the way to Jack Jones's place. His landlady was outside, humming to herself as she swept debris into the street. When she glanced up, Easter was marching toward her.

"Jack there?" Easter screeched, clutching her fists to her chest. The woman shook her head no and watched as Easter turned and streaked back in the direction she'd come.

By the time she arrived at the UNIA headquarters the muscles in her legs were twitching. She took the stone steps two at a time and pressed the black doorbell and jumped back in surprise when the firecracker sound of a gunshot echoed from behind the double doors, instead of the *ding-dong-dang* she'd expected.

Colin was already in the building when Easter discovered their life savings was gone. He had a snub-nosed .38 shoved deep into his right pants pocket, the stock certificates in his left. A sheath of sweat lay across his forehead and the short metal neck of the gun had begun to pulsate and burn hot against his thigh.

The building was always filled with people and Colin was a familiar and friendly face, so nobody took special notice of him when he entered the busy office located in the front parlor.

A typist named Gail Forbes looked up from her stack of papers and acknowledged him with a slight nod of her head. A man at the desk across from hers hollered, "How you doing, Colin?" then used his eraser to rub out a number on the ledger page he was working on.

"Is Marcus here?" Colin's voice came across louder than he meant it to, and the room went quiet for a moment. Colin tightened his hand around the wooden handle of the gun and forced a nervous smile. "I—I got an appointment with him," he said in a lower tone.

"Upstairs," someone finally responded.

He turned awkwardly around, colliding first with a coat rack and then a file cabinet. Someone called out, "You sick, man?"

Kendrick Lawrence was coming down the stairway when Colin grabbed hold of the banister and placed his foot on the bottom step. Kendrick said, "Hey, man," and almost stepped aside to allow Colin to pass, but he saw the gleam of perspiration on his face and the odd, vacant look in his eyes and an alarm sounded in his head. Kendrick gripped Colin's shoulder, and his hand almost recoiled from the moist material. "Hey, Gibbs, where you going?"

Colin addressed his shoes: "Up to see him."

Kendrick saw that Colin was shaking and panic

immediately swept through him. "Uhm, why don't you wait here and I'll go fetch him for you."

Colin nodded and mumbled, "Yeah, okay."

Kendrick considered him for a moment, and when he turned around Colin punched him in the kidney. Bright lights exploded behind Kendrick's pupils and he sank down to his knees. Colin leapt over him and bounded up the stairs.

"Stop him!" Kendrick yelled just as Marcus Garvey and another man appeared on the top landing.

Colin pulled the gun from his pocket, pointed, and pulled the trigger. The bullet ricocheted off the wall and grazed Marcus's temple. The second bullet caught him in the arm, and he collapsed against the wall.

Colin aimed again but was tackled by Kendrick and two other men, allowing Garvey to escape into the safety of his office. The mass of bodies struggled, punches were thrown, and the men tumbled down the steps and ended in a heap at the bottom. The gun went skating across the parquet floor, and when Colin reached out to retrieve it a young woman whacked his hand with a law book and then brought it down square on the top of his head. Colin collapsed into darkness.

When it was over, thirteen of the banister spokes were splintered, the pier glass in the front foyer was shattered, and the stock certificates Colin had purchased a year earlier were strewn across the floor.

The sound of the gunshot startled Easter and she turned and bolted down the steps, out into traffic, and across the street to safety. Moments later the doors flung open and a man darted from the building, frantically waving his hands and screaming, "Police! Police!" as he tore down the sidewalk. It seemed an eternity passed before he returned with two police officers, who pushed him aside as they pulled guns from their holsters. One officer crouched down at the foot of the steps while the other sprinted into the house. After a moment the second officer followed.

Out on the street people began to gather, and more officers arrived, accompanied by a paddy wagon. Barricades were put in place and batons were waved. A horse-drawn ambulance arrived and then Marcus Garvey appeared in the doorway, his dark face splattered with blood. He stood erect as a soldier and waved at the crowd who erupted in applause. Marcus gave his onlookers a hearty thumbs-up and another cheer went up. Two UNIA officers helped him into the waiting ambulance and he was whisked safely away.

The assailant appeared, his head bowed and his wrists cuffed at his back. Two brawny policemen stood on either side of him, their hands wrapped tight around his arms. They yanked him down the steps, toward the paddy wagon. Easter stood on the tips of her toes. The crowd booed and hissed. Colin raised his head; his eyes swept over the angry gathering and stopped briefly on the astounded face of his wife.

The news whipped through Harlem like wild fire and landed in the ear of Meredith's cook who was buying tomatoes at a vegetable stand. He carried it back to the penthouse and delivered it to the butler, who chuckled as he stood polishing a silver teapot.

"Is he dead?"

"I think so," answered the cook.

When the girl named Dolly, whose job it was to attend to the immediate needs of the mistress of the house, and who was, to the butler's disdain, a devoted Garveyite, strolled into the dining area, the butler raised his head and gleefully proclaimed, "Your Black Moses has been slain!"

Rain was lounging in the music room when she heard the butler's declaration and the bile and anguish in Dolly's response, and so decided to take a walk and find out for herself if the rumor had legs.

Minutes after Colin was thrown into the dank cell at the Harlem jail, Jack Jones walked into the aftermath of the melee. UNIA members were scurrying about tidying up and assessing the damage. Jack stepped gingerly over the jagged pieces of mirrored glass and wood and sidled up to the shaken woman who had dealt the crippling blow.

"What happened here?"

Valerie Cumberbatch raised her large brown eyes and Jack saw that they were swimming with tears. "He . . . he had a gun," she managed in a trembling voice.

"Who did?"

"Colin . . . Colin Gibbs."

She broke down in sobs and Jack reached out and patted her shoulder. "It's okay, take your time," he heard himself say, then realized he'd uttered those same words a million times as a police officer in D.C.

"Did he . . . ?" Jack didn't want to hear himself ask the question.

A shiver went through Valerie's body. "He shot at Marcus and . . ." The sobbing started up again and this time it didn't seem as if she would be able to regain control. But time was of the essence.

"Is he dead?" Jack asked anxiously. Val shook her head no and Jack was happy that her tears blurred the disappointment shining on his face.

Colin had been an easy target; his growing unhappiness with his wife, his financial situation, and the lack of return on his investment in Marcus Garvey's Black Star Line had fed his discontent until it began to spill out of him like sewage.

Jack had played his role of the good friend, confidant, and understanding black brother to the hilt. He'd lent his ear whenever Colin needed someone to listen and nodded sympathetically in all the right places. In Jack's tiny rented room he and Colin had played cards and drank until the wee hours of the morning as Jack carefully voiced his own suspicions about Marcus Garvey. He had to be delicate because Colin had great respect for Marcus and his ideals, respect that ran root deep. But blood was thicker than water, so when Colin's mother became ill and he tried to speak to Marcus about buying back the stock shares, the leader had deftly avoided him and Colin's frustration became radiant.

Jack Jones used that and liquor to slowly twist Colin's mind.

"I could kill 'em!" Colin slurred drunkenly one night.

"I'm sure one day someone will," Jack offered matter-of-factly.

Colin glared at him, "Not one day and someone—me, tomorrow!"

Jack's heart flapped, but his face remained solemn.

"You think I'm making sport?" Colin challenged.

"Aren't you?"

Colin jumped to his feet and trained his index finger on Jack. "If I had a gun I would put a bullet right between those black eyes of his."

"Sit down," Jack chuckled. "You're drunk."

Colin's bottom lip hung recklessly from his face. "That may be, but a drunk tongue speaks a sober mind," he said, as he dropped down into the chair and reached for the glass of whiskey.

"If you're serious," Jack whispered, "I mean really serious, I can get you a gun."

Colin stared at him for a moment and then waved his hand.

"*You think I'm making sport?*" Jack mocked Colin's Carribean colloquialism.

Colin laughed, reached over the table, and patted Jack heartily on the head. "Did I ever tell you," he said as he refilled his glass, "that you look like the white people in my country?"

Jack nodded his head, "Yes, all the time."

Colin drained his glass and poured another. Jack watched him.

"So, do you want me to get you the gun or not?"

Colin's head lolled to one side and he wrapped his arms around himself like a blanket. A foolish grin spread across his face and he dropped his head back on his neck. "I'ma give that black bastard one more chance," he mumbled, "and then bang, he's dead." Colin chuckled before dozing off.

Jack would have to devise a plan that would force

Colin's hand. He was, after all, a man on the edge; Jack would just have to find the one thing that would send him careening over it. And after a few days thought he finally found it.

The telegram was bogus.

But Colin didn't know that and now he sat in a jail cell with a tray of food resting on the floor at his feet. He looked at the brick walls, breathed in the rank bouquet, and knew that this was not one of his dreams. The telegram had arrived and he'd read the saddest words ever written: *Your mother is dead.*

And at that moment the only thing deeper than his grief was his hatred for Marcus Garvey and so he'd marched off to find Jack Jones and the gun he said he could get him and then he'd gone to the UNIA with blood in his eyes.

Colin dropped his head into his hands and began to sob.

The day passed into night and then day again and no one came to see him. Not a lawyer and not his wife. He glanced up at the small window, at the slate-colored sky and thought, *Even God has turned His back on me.*

Halfway through the second day, two officers appeared beyond the bars and ordered him to his feet. "Back against the wall," one of them barked. That same one aimed his pistol at Colin's heart while the other unlocked the door, stepped in, and ordered him to turn around and face the wall. Colin did as he was told and the officer cuffed his wrists and ankles.

The Harlem Station was circular in structure. In its former life, the building had been used for storing, grading, and exporting wheat. The space of floor between the cells and the edge of the balcony was narrow, which made it difficult for the three men to walk side-by-side. So one of the officers fell to the rear.

The newspapers would report that Colin had made an attempt to escape. That in his desperate state of mind, he had broken free of the officers, climbed up onto the short wall of the balcony, spread his arms out at his sides like wings, and leapt to his death. That story, just like the telegram, was a lie.

The policemen ushered Colin across the wood plank floors, their rings of keys clinking loudly and echoing off the walls. Colin shuffled slowly down the dim corridor; his heart raced in his chest and thumped like a drum in his ears. The air changed and was suddenly swathed with the scent of bougainvillea. Colin thought his mind was getting away from him, but with each step the perfume grew more pungent. He came to an abrupt stop, raised his head, closed his eyes, and inhaled. Visions of home appeared and Colin smiled. "Do you smell that?" he murmured.

The two officers exchanged perplexed glances and then the one in the rear frowned, shrugged his shoulders, and rested his hand on the crown of Colin's head. The other he wrapped around Colin's chin and with great force pulled each hand in opposite directions, severing Colin's skull from his neck with a pop. Colin fell to the floor like a rag doll. They hoisted his limp body over the edge of the balcony; before either of them could look away, Colin hit the floor with a sickening clap.

Easter had not been permitted to see him at the jail.

When she asked why, the sergeant in charge said, "I have my orders." And then ordered her to go home and advised that if she refused, "I'll throw your black ass in a cell right next to your husband."

At the morgue Colin's body was displayed on a table of steel. The smile was still pressed against his lips and when Easter looked at him a sea of emotion rose up in her throat and she slapped her hands over her mouth. She signed the papers that needed to be signed, including the one that stated that Colin's body could not be released to her because even though he was her husband, he was not an American but a British subject who had committed a crime in the United States, making him a criminal of the state and the country, which qualified him—dead or alive—for deportation.

Easter kissed his smiling mouth, slipped the silver wedding band from his finger and spent the next three hours weeping and walking aimlessly around the city. Her grief was bottomless, and even though the streets teemed with people, she felt alone in the world. When she finally rounded the corner of her block, she looked up and saw Rain standing there, the ends of her bright yellow scarf fluttering in the late-afternoon breeze. Rain lifted her hand into the air. It was not a greeting but a show of unity that said, *You are not alone—I am here.*

CHAPTER 21

In 1922 everything changed again. The Eskimo pie was invented; James Joyce's *Ulysses* was printed in Paris; snow fell on Mauna Loa, Hawaii; Babe Ruth signed a three-year contract with the New York Yankees; Eugene O'Neill was awarded the Pulitzer Prize for Drama; Frederick Douglass's home was dedicated as a national shrine; former heavyweight champion of the world Jack Johnson invented the wrench; and James Wormley "Jack" Jones was recognized by a former D.C. police officer as he sat in Chumley's staring down at his cup of coffee.

"Jack?"

Jack looked up and into the dark face hovering over him.

"Jack Jones, right?"

Jack nodded his head as he tried to place the face.

"Benjamin Caruthers," the man said and sat down. "We worked together in D.C."

Jack's lips quivered.

"Wow, it's been ages," Benjamin said and presented his hand. Jack took it and they shook. "You still a cop?"

Jack's eyes wandered around the bar. People were looking. And those who weren't looking were listening.

"Uhm, no, I'm not."

"Me neither man," Benjamin's voice boomed. "So, how's the wife and kids?"

Jack's life spilled out of Benjamin's mouth, like water from a spout. Every detail of who he really was: a former police officer, husband and father, with a house and mortgage in Maryland.

Jack looked around the bar; it was filled with mostly whites, but that didn't make Jack feel safe—Garvey had plenty of white sympathizers, nigger lovers, Negrophiles— they were everywhere, and the news that Jack Jones, one of Garvey's most trusted officers, was not at all who he claimed to be arrived at Garvey's doorstep wrapped in a red bow.

Within twenty-four hours a special edition of Garvey's newspaper, *The Negro World*, hit the streets of Harlem. The front page showed a picture of Jack Jones; below that, in bold print, was the word *JUDAS*.

That of course ended Jack's career as the first ever Negro FBI agent. To tell the truth, James Wormley "Jack" Jones was relieved. He returned to Washington, D.C., handed his gun and badge to his superior, and in return received a handshake and a plaque acknowledging his years of service. And just like that he became James Wormley "Jack" Jones, civilian.

Later that year, Mussolini marched on Rome; the architect Howard Carter entered King Tut's tomb; the British court sentenced Mahatma Gandhi to six years in prison; Eubie Blake and Noble Sissi's all-Negro musical *Shuffle Along* premiered on Broadway; Easter was working full time as a laundress and publishing stories in *The Crisis* magazine under the moniker E.V. Gibbs; Harcourt, Brace & Company published Claude McKay's book of poetry *Harlem Shadows*; and the Harlem Renaissance began.

BOOK III
NEGROPHILIA

CHAPTER 22

Easter arrived on time, dressed in a lime-green taffeta dress she'd borrowed from Mattie Mae–now-Madeline. The dress fit her all wrong; it was too tight across her middle and too large at the top. Madeline had watched with great amusement as Easter squeezed herself into a girdle and then padded the inside of her bra with toilet paper.

Meredith staged the terrace of her penthouse to resemble a Grecian hall, complete with scrolled columns and topiaries of mythical creatures. Servers wore togas and carried silver trays laden with all varieties of delectable offerings.

The party was given in Easter's honor. She'd become a regular contributor to *The Crisis*, and with each story her popularity with the readers had grown.

Easter moved among the attendees practically unnoticed. She would pause next to groups of people and slyly eavesdrop on their conversations about the explosion of literature flowing out of Harlem. Her heart fluttered excitedly when she came across a gentleman who exclaimed with great exhilaration, "This E.V. Gibbs is something special. Did you read the story "Parliament Road"? It was stunning!"

Easter grinned.

"Escargot, miss?" asked a tall, blond-haired, blue-eyed waiter whose body had been slathered in Max Factor Grease Paint #32 bestowing him with a Mediterranean glow. Easter peered down at the murky-colored balls of flesh. They didn't appear at all appetizing.

"Escargot?" Easter repeated stupidly. She had no idea what it was. A devilish smile crept over the young man's face and he leaned over and whispered, "Snails."

Easter went gray, shook her head, and hurried to the other side of the balcony where a cluster of people stood chatting. Meredith and her husband Eduardo were at the center of the group. Easter stepped behind a column out of sight.

They were a breathtaking, strikingly attractive couple. Movie-star beautiful; Goldwyn-Mayer couldn't have paired a better romantic duo if it tried.

"Merry, where do you come up with these fantastic tales?" An elegantly adorned Negro woman draped in black silk and dripping with jewels laughed and wagged her index finger at Meredith.

"Oh, A'Lelia, you know it's all true, darling. It happened at your house!"

The crowd melted into laughter and A'Lelia shook her head in mock dismay.

"*Carlo*," Meredith reached past her husband and took hold of Carl Van Vechten's wrist, "you remember, don't you, darling, A'Lelia inviting us over for dinner and serving us hog maws and bathtub gin in the kitchen while Langston, Wallace, and Zora ate roast duck and drank champagne in that grand dining room of hers?"

Carl smiled mischievously and dragged his palm over his slick blond mane. "I don't remember that gathering, Merry. Are you sure I was there?" He winked at A'Lelia.

"Oh you!" Meredith squealed and dropped his hand. "You are such a scamp!"

The group howled with laughter.

"I'm going to have to say goodnight," A'Lelia suddenly announced.

"Already? But you've only just arrived," Merry pouted.

"I've been here for two whole hours."

"You know A'Lelia does not stay out long. We're lucky to have had her for this amount of time," Carl said as he linked his arm with A'Lelia's. "I'll accompany you to your car."

A'Lelia bid the group goodnight and turned to leave. When she was out of earshot, Meredith whispered, "Poor thing, she has such bad feet, they swell horribly."

The others nodded sympathetically.

A few moments later Meredith looked up to see Rain strutting toward her.

"Rain!" Meredith's shrill voice cut through the night air. "You are fashionably late as always!"

An irritated look passed across Eduardo's face.

The two women hugged.

"I must say, darling, you look delicious!"

Rain beamed. "Thank you, Merry, and might I pay you the same compliment?"

"Why, darling, if you don't I might never speak to you again!"

They laughed.

"Easter, for heaven's sake, what are you doing hiding behind that shrub?" Merry cried.

Easter cringed and stepped guiltily out into the open. Rain walked over, took her by the hand, and led her to the center of the group. "This is whom you've all come to meet." Meredith squeezed Easter's hand. "Easter . . . I mean, E.V. Gibbs."

They showered her with a dozen hellos, followed by just as many hands that reached out to shake hers. Meredith made the introductions. There were so many people; Easter knew she would never remember every name.

After too many glasses of champagne, Easter finally slipped away to a quiet section of the patio. She was giddy and she swayed unsteadily on her feet as she stood gazing at the bright city lights. She was humming to herself when a handsome, brown-skinned man approached her.

"I'm so glad to get you all to myself," he said as he fished out a pack of cigarettes, shook one free, and offered it to Easter.

She thanked him and slipped it between her lips.

"My pleasure," he said, lighting first her cigarette and then his own. He blew a cloud of smoke into the air and they watched it evaporate. "I wanted to congratulate you on your success and tell you how much I've been enjoying your writing."

A waiter stepped between them. "Cake?"

Her companion gingerly plucked the square of three-layer confection from the tray. His eyes sparkled as he watched the waiter glide away. In that moment his face took on a soft dreamy quality and when he looked in Easter's direction again, he seemed surprised to see her standing there.

"I'm sorry, you were saying?"

Easter laughed, "I wasn't saying a thing."

The man grinned sheepishly, pondered for a moment, and then presented his hand. "I just wanted to introduce myself and tell you that I think you have a great voice. I look forward to reading more of your work."

Easter placed her hand in his. "And you are?"

"Didn't I say?"

Easter shook her head.

"Langston. Langston Hughes."

At around 2 a.m. the crowd began to thin. Groups of people bid their goodbyes, most of whom had no intention of calling it a night. Private cars and hansom cabs collected the guests and then deposited them at the Cotton Club, Bamboo Inn, the Renaissance Casino, and the Savoy.

Those who remained at 409 Edgecombe Avenue were treated to a raucous session of down-home dirty blues from Gladys Bentley, who'd arrived dressed in her signature top hat and tails. When she eased her 250-pound frame down on onto the piano bench, the legs shook. She stroked and pounded the keys of Meredith's Gerhard Heintzman baby grand piano, and belted out raunchy lyrics. The guests caught a second wind, and Lindy Hopped until dawn.

Easter pushed her way through the revelers, through the French doors, and into the main parlor where she had to step over a man and woman splayed out drunk on the floor. As she moved along, she came across more of the same; there were bodies everywhere, the parlor looked like a killing field. She continued unsteadily down the hall, unsure, in her drunken state, exactly which bed-room belonged to Rain. And so she went from room to room pushing open doors and calling out her friend's name.

Behind one door she found a woman on her knees, her head hidden between the thick thighs of a man Easter recalled meeting earlier in the evening. The next door she tried revealed the butler standing before a full-length mirror, naked save for the expensive nylons and garter belt he wore. Caught by surprise, he reached for his hairbrush and threw it angrily at her.

Easter stumbled along, giggling at the madness surrounding her. She turned another doorknob, peered into the room, and recognized Rain's silk robe tossed across the bed. Easter stepped in and pulled the door shut behind her. She kicked off her shoes, ran across the plush carpet, and swan dived onto the king bed.

The sound of running water cackled beyond the bathroom door. "Can you believe it? All of this for me?" Easter hugged herself. "You hear me, girl? . . . Rain," she called as she climbed off the bed.

When she stood up the blood rushed rapidly from her head and she crumpled to the floor laughing, and commenced to crawl to the bathroom.

"Rain?" Easter squinted through the steam. "You hear me—"

The vision hurdled Easter back in time, back to the tent, back to the kiss that drove a stake through her heart. There were Meredith and Rain, standing naked in the tub, wrapped in a lovers' embrace beneath the spray of water.

Easter did not remember charging at them, arms

wheeling like propellers. Nor did she recall them trying to fend her off but failing, and slipping on the smooth porcelain belly of the tub, and crashing into a heap. She did not remember walking down the hallway, or the scent of Eduardo's cigar, or his wide startled eyes. She did remember the walls turning into custard and the floor breaking away beneath her feet and the stink of her vomit as it spewed from her mouth.

When she woke up the next evening in one of the many spare rooms, Rain was sitting at her bedside. Easter felt angry and ashamed, but Rain patted her hand like an understanding mother and said, "Girl, you gonna have to shake those feelings for me." And then she pointed to the blue and green shiner under her left eye. "Or one of us going to end up dead."

Her voice was filled with humor, but the seriousness of the matter was bright in her eyes.

Easter whispered, "Did I do that?"

Rain nodded her head. "You think I don't love you. But I do. I love you with all my heart." She softly thumped her chest. "Cause I sleep with Meredith don't mean that I love her more, it just mean that we light a fire in one another that we can't control. That's all."

Easter tried to turn her head away, but Rain caught her by the chin and held it firm.

"Like the fire Colin lit in you." She paused and searched Easter's face for some understanding. "You don't light that particular type of fire in me. You light a different fire. Don't you see how I glow when you walk in the room? You calming to me like a easy summer day, you my rock, Easter, don't you know that?"

Easter didn't even try to fight back the tears.

"What you and I have, Meredith and I will never have. Me and you," Rain pointed at herself and then turned her finger back on Easter, "we ace boon coons forever."

CHAPTER 23

The *Daily Tattler*, the gossip rag of the era, printed a story that cast Meredith in the most ghastly of lights. It claimed that she—Meredith Tomas—the beautiful and elegant socialite wife of the wealthy Cuban tobacco maverick—Eduardo Tomas—had gone off to Atlantic City and wed the openly homosexual, chocolate-colored, piano-playing blues singer Gladys Bentley. A photograph accompanied the glaring headline. It had been snapped months earlier at the party thrown in Easter's honor. The scandalous photograph pictured Meredith seated on Gladys's lap, her arms thrown provocatively around Gladys's neck, their lips just millimeters apart.

Someone, no one knew who, had inserted a copy of the *Tattler* between the pages of Eduardo's regular morning paper, and placed it on the breakfast table next to his cup of coffee. Eduardo sat down, lit a cigarette, took three quick sips of his coffee, and picked up the newspaper. The gossip rag slid out and onto the table. Meredith and Gladys had made the front page.

When Meredith strolled into the room, she didn't spot the *Tattler* resting on his plate, and failed to notice the rage on his face. When Meredith bent to give Eduardo his morning kiss, he pulled his arm back as far as it would go and brought it forward with such ferocity that when his palm made contact with her cheek, the blow lifted her out of her slippers and sent her flying across the room into the buffet. When the butler peeked out from behind the kitchen door, Meredith was cradling her cheek and crawling along the floorboards.

"*Lesbiana! Lesbiana!*" Eduardo screeched as he stormed through the apartment toward Rain's bedroom. He kicked in the door, snatched the sleeping Rain from the bed, and bounced her against the wall, stunning her into submission. When Meredith reached the parlor, Eduardo was dragging Rain across the floor toward the butler who was smiling smugly as he dutifully unbolted the locks of the front door.

Eduardo tossed Rain out into the hallway like common trash and then returned to his breakfast. The butler poured him a fresh cup of coffee and Meredith sat quietly watching the square of butter melt slowly away on her toast.

A month later Eduardo stepped off the train in Detroit and sucked in the biting cold Michigan air. His mistress Anna rushed across the platform, threw her arms around his neck, and showered his face with kisses. Eduardo opened his mouth to speak, but instead took his last breath, and dropped dead right where he stood.

When the news reached Meredith she was sitting in the drawing room of her lavish apartment, lazily filing her nails and wondering about dinner. Dolly entered, handed her the telegram, and Meredith used the metal fingernail file to slice open the envelope. She read the telegram three times before folding the paper and sliding it back into the envelope. She dropped the envelope onto the sofa table, retrieved the nail file, and resumed her task, with a small, satisfied smile resting on her lips.

The repast was an extravagant affair. Because red was Eduardo's favorite color, Meredith wore a ruby chiffon dress embellished with elaborate beadwork, complete with a trailing sash. She hired the Cuban bandleader Xavier Cugat to provide the music. The menu consisted of black bean salad, empanadas, mango bread, fried platanos, arroz con pollo, roasted pork, and shrimp casserole.

A reporter from the *Daily Tattler* bribed her way in and the next day recounted the spectacle for her dedicated readers:

> As Eduardo Tomas's coffin sat on the 42nd Street pier, waiting to be hoisted onto the steamer Alabama, which sailed for Cuba that night, his widow Meredith Tomas celebrated his demise in grand style. Meredith and her guests ate, drank, and cha-cha'd late into the night.
>
> Rumor has it that Meredith stands to inherit six million clams as a result of her husband's death.
>
> Six million?
>
> Well I guess that is something to celebrate—but she could have at least pretended like she was going to miss him!

Meredith finished reading the piece, folded the paper, and flung it across the room where it landed on the floor at the butler's feet.

"They say such nasty things about me," she whined as she whipped her celery stick around her Bloody Mary.

"Easter, nobody wrote garish things about you when your husband . . . umm . . ." Meredith struggled to find the right word. "Died."

Easter looked up from her plate of poached eggs and bacon and said, "Just ignore it, Meredith."

After Eduardo tossed Rain out into the hall and onto the streets, she'd gone to stay with Easter. Meredith went to visit as often as she could and Easter would allow them their privacy, leaving them alone in the apartment while she took long walks through Harlem. During those outings her mind wandered over her life, her family, and Colin, and sometimes the memories pressed down on her and left her wet-eyed and blue. In order to shake the funk she and Rain would go to the cabarets to drink and sing along to the bawdy songs as they danced, flinging their hands up into the air and viciously thrusting their hips this way and that as if the very movement could rid them of their miseries.

Eduardo's death was a shock to everyone and Rain and Easter rushed to their friend's side. Meredith cried and told them that she couldn't be alone, she needed them to be there with her or else she didn't know what she might do. And so Rain moved back in and Easter came along too.

When word got out that Easter had moved to 409 Edgecombe Avenue—the place where no other Negro lived as far as anyone knew—the women at the laundry where she worked looked at Easter and asked themselves, *Why her?* No matter how many times they bathed, the smell of detergent clung stubbornly to their hair and skin, yet Easter arrived every day smelling of expensive perfume.

Why did she continue to work there? Was it to rub their faces in her happiness and good fortune? Was she some kind of sadist? Maybe, they mused over their mid-day cigarettes, she needed to come. After all she was Meredith Tomas's *girl*, wasn't she? Maybe Meredith Tomas loaned Easter out to the laundry the way whites had loaned their slaves out to other plantations.

"Is it true," one stout woman asked in a mocking tone, "that she keeps you locked in a gilded cage, and that you perform tricks for her guests?"

Easter rolled her eyes.

Another said, "So you think you better than me because you can read and write?"

She didn't think that at all.

Easter tried not to take it personal, she understood why they taunted and ridiculed her the way they did—it distracted them from their own sorrows.

But if they knew the realities of her life at 409 Edgecombe, those women would have pressed their lips together and swallowed their nasty remarks because they all knew what it felt like to love someone who loved someone else. It was like eating ground glass.

At 409 Edgecombe Avenue, Easter stuck her fingers in her ears and hummed the national anthem when the sounds of Meredith and Rain's lovemaking echoed down the hallway and clamored at her bedroom door. When they gazed lovingly into one another's eyes or touched in an intimate way, Easter averted her gaze to the blades of sunshine cutting across the hardwood floors. The effort it took to contain her emotions often left her melancholy and agitated. But God was not always unkind and every now and again justice was done, when Meredith would look up from whatever it was she was doing, touch the pad of her index finger to her chin, and coyly announce, "I think I'm in the mood for Chinese tonight."

Chinese did not mean cuisine; it was Meredith's code word for her desire to be with a man. Rain would bristle and charge from the room. And it was during those times that the stake in Easter's heart would pull back a bit and she would watch with glee as Rain was relegated to standing in her shoes; Easter hoped to God they pinched.

CHAPTER 24

Meredith had a fondness for other people's things. When the apartment was empty, she took great pleasure in rifling through the personal belongings of her guests and staff. In the butler's room she found silk nylons and a pair of panties hidden beneath his mattress and laughed until her sides hurt. Her maid Dolly had nothing of great interest, just a Bible with the names and birth dates of family members written neatly on the last page, a birthday card from a long ago suitor, and a sepia-toned picture of her mother, dead six years by the time she came under Meredith's employ.

Rain's treasures included countless silk scarves in all the colors of the rainbow, playbills, a bag of reefer, a letter addressed to someone named Vaughn that was scrawled in the crude hand of a three-year-old and riddled with misspellings and bad grammar.

It was in Easter's room that she found the best treasure, a gem of a story still in its infancy about a girl named Nora. It was the most exquisite writing that Meredith had read in several years and she wondered why Easter hadn't shared it with her, hadn't even asked for her guidance—not that the story needed it. Meredith sat on the floor, folded her legs Indian-style, read and reread passages, and wondered how such loveliness and perfection had come out of someone so plain . . . so very, very average. Yes, Easter was a wonderful storyteller, but this . . . Meredith ran her fingers along the passages of typed print and began to seethe with jealousy . . . this was a far cry from Easter's previous works. It was, in a word, exceptional.

A daily check found that the story was at a standstill. Not one new word had been written in days, and Meredith was eager for more.

"How's the writing coming?" Meredith ventured casually one day.

"It's on and off."

Meredith eyed her. "Mostly on," she said as she reached over and plucked a cube of sugar from the crystalware, "or mostly off?"

Easter scratched at her scalp. "Depends on the day, I guess."

Meredith dropped the cube into her coffee. "It's the work. It wears you out and you come home too tired to write."

Easter thought about it for a moment. "I suppose that could be it."

"I want you to quit that job at the laundry," Meredith announced wistfully. "I've been thinking a lot about this and I just don't see how you can concentrate on your writing if you're toiling away in that awful place ten hours a day."

Easter opened her mouth to speak, but Meredith raised her hand.

"You don't have to worry about money, I'll provide that." Then she added pointedly, "I'll be your *benefactor*."

Meredith loved the title: Benefactor. She had been

called many things—daughter, wife, philanthropist, humanitarian, and widow—but never benefactor. The title fit her perfectly. She repeated it and the word rang in her ears as if shouted by a million people.

Langston Hughes had Carl Van Vechten, Zora Neale Hurston had Charlotte Osgood, and now E.V. Gibbs would have Meredith Tomas. The world was wonderful again.

"Are you sure?" Easter asked.

Meredith cupped Easter's face in her hands and said, "More than sure."

Nothing to do but eat, sleep, and write. It took some getting used to and at first the words came in drips and drabs, like an old pipe being coaxed by a plumber's wrench. October was upon her and the sidewalks were littered with autumn leaves and still nothing. Weeks passed and two new moons and then winter smiled its icy grin, and with the first December snow the words finally came.

CHAPTER 25

Even those white people who claimed to love all things African and wore the title *Negrophile* like a badge of honor on their lapels—even those people were taken aback by the actions of Nancy Cunard, the heir to the multimillion-dollar Cunard Line shipping company.

Nancy's mother, Maude Alice Burke, had heard from the mouths of various busybodies that her daughter was cavorting around Europe with Negroes. Negroes!

Maude attributed Nancy's obvious mental breakdown to a growing addiction to absinthe—at least that's what she told her friends in order to save face. She sent word to Nancy demanding the end of her ridiculous, embarrassing, and reckless behavior and ordered home forthwith. If Nancy disobeyed, Maude would have no choice but to strike her name permanently from her will and her life.

Nancy's response to her mother's threats and outrage was to hop a steamer heading to America with her Negro lover, the Chicago-born musician Henry Coward, standing steadfastly by her side.

For Henry, Nancy had been just another white face in a white world. The two had met in Paris at a club he and his band were performing at. Nancy was so enthused by his music that after the set she invited him to join her for a drink. They enjoyed a lively discussion about music and America, after which he'd thanked her for her kindness and conversation and returned to the stage. Some nights later, when she showed up again, he did not even remember her. She looked to him like all the other white women who frequented the club.

Henry did not know that Nancy was an heiress until the second time they slept together. When his band members found out that he was seeing a white woman—and a rich one at that—they took him to the pub and demanded he buy them a round of drinks.

"Careful now," one of them warned, "white women have been known to lose their minds over black dick."

Henry assured them that he had the situation under control, and that Nancy was just something *to do* while he was in Paris. "I do have a wife back home in Chicago, you know," he reminded them with a laugh, and then used Nancy's money to buy three more rounds.

When Nancy announced that she wanted to go to America, to Harlem specifically, Henry said, "Have a good time." But when she added that she wanted him to accompany her, he immediately felt the scratchy fibers of a lynch rope against his neck. "No, I can't do that."

"Why not?"

"Because America is not Europe and Harlem is not Paris. We will not be able to stroll hand-in-hand down the streets in New York without being harassed, or worse."

Nancy blinked. "Worse?"

"I could get killed," Henry stated bluntly.

But she wore him down with pleading and money

and the promise of an automobile, and so he acquiesced, and the noose around his neck pulled tighter.

They arrived in New York just before Christmas; the city was brimming with holiday cheer and the air was heavy with the aroma of roasting chestnuts. Carolers roamed the streets, garland was wound around lampposts, wreathes hung in windows, and mistletoe was tacked above doorways.

Nancy hired a private car, and Henry directed the driver through the vilest of Negro ghettoes, pointing out from behind the safety of the sedan windows the degradation the white man had levied on the colored masses. Nancy's eyes welled with water.

When they arrived at 409 Edgecombe Avenue Easter noted that Henry was handsome and had a soft, quiet way about him. Nancy was a statuesque and reed thin with eager, darting eyes. Her conversation rushed out in gusts, and she used her hands in an exaggerated fashion. On her wrists she wore intricately carved wooden bangles, stacked up to her elbows.

"Your bracelets are beautiful," Easter said. "Where did you get them?"

"The Ivory Coast." Nancy slipped one massive bangle from her wrist and handed it to Easter. "A gift from me to you." She cleared her throat. "Henry," Nancy explained as she rested a delicate hand on his knee, "was my introduction to the world of the Negro. Before our encounter, I had never even spoken to a Negro. They were invisible to me and now I see them everywhere!"

Easter and Rain exchanged glances.

Meredith nodded. "So, darling, what brings you to New York?"

"I'm here to collect material for an anthology I'm working on."

"An anthology?" Meredith leaned forward. "Do tell!"

"It's a collection of stories, poetry, and essays written by and about Negroes from all around the globe. This is something that has never been done before."

"Sounds lovely, darling. Who's committed?"

"W.E.B. DuBois has already submitted an essay entitled 'Black America' and I have a number of pieces from Zora Neale Hurston. Maude Cuney Hare has written a tantalizing prospective called 'The Folk Music of the Creoles.'" Nancy trembled with excitement.

"What an impressive list of participants. What are you going to call it?"

Nancy took a deep breath. "I'm going to call it *Negro*," she announced proudly.

Rain giggled into her glass of gin and Easter thought she'd heard wrong.

Meredith gave Nancy a cool look. "Really?" she said smugly. "Carlo is working on a book with a similar title." She tapped her finger against her glass as she struggled to remember. "Ah, yes," she said with a snap of her fingers, "his book is called *Nigger Heaven*."

Nancy went pale. "Meredith," she hissed, her eyes bouncing between Rain and Easter's faces, "that is a horrible, disgusting word."

"What is?"

Henry had wandered off to the music room and was playing the piano. At the sound of the word he'd missed a note and begun the score from the beginning.

"*Nigger*," Nancy whispered. "It's the vilest word in the English language and I don't understand how it's used so freely here in this country. It's bounced around like a child's ball. And to use it in literature, in the very thing that *should* bring the races together . . ." Nancy shook her head in dismay. "Well, I think it's just awful."

Meredith was unfazed because she understood that as unsavory as the word was, it was also a part of life, a stitch in the American quilt. One would have to go back hundreds of years to rid the world of it and everyone knew the past could not be undone, so the word, as far as Meredith was concerned, was here to stay.

But she humored Nancy: "Darling, you are absolutely right." Her eyes swung to Easter and then back to Nancy. "Did I tell you that Easter is also working on a book?"

Nancy grinned. "Oh my, I had no idea that you were a writer."

"Oh yes, and a very talented one. In fact, I'm her benefactor!"

Nancy's eyes flashed. "Really? I would love to read some of your work."

"Yes," Rain added, beaming admiringly at Easter, "she is a wonderful writer."

Meredith's head reeled around. "And how would you know? You can't even read."

The statement was unexpected and certainly un-provoked. The room fell silent and Rain, never one to be struck speechless, shot Meredith a wounded look, pressed herself deep into the sofa cushions, and did not utter another word for the rest of the night. Easter looked down at her hands in shame and an embarrassed Nancy fumbled nervously with the pineapple-shaped stopper of the crystal decanter until it came free with a pop. Only then was the spell broken.

The afternoon melted into evening, Henry continued to play the piano, and at the end of the night, when the couple gathered themselves to leave, the butler helped Nancy into her full-length fox fur, but did not make a move to offer the same assistance to Henry. As Henry shrugged on his gray, brushed-wool coat, Easter noted its mink collar and for some reason likened it to a dog collar or the metal bracelets owners fastened to the legs of their expensive birds.

CHAPTER 26

Horace Liveright was at this time one of New York's most prominent publishers. His house, Boni & Liveright, had published many previously unknown writers to great fame. T.S. Eliot, William Faulkner, and Ernest Hemingway owed him a debt of gratitude. Horace opposed censorship and possessed a deep and fiery love for the arts, theater in particular. He supported that conviction with his own money, which he used to finance a number of stage productions. Some did well; many others did not.

A tall man with wise eyes and smooth skin, he had an ardor for excess that was apparent in the sheer amounts of alcohol he consumed and the lavish parties he hosted that often went on for days at a time.

In attendance at one of those parties was the publisher Alfred Harcourt, who had never been any good at holding his liquor. Alcohol of any kind or amount, even the tiniest bit syringed into the middle of a chocolate candy, affected him. So needless to say, after two gin gimlets Alfred's drunk tongue spoke his sober mind and he told Horace the very thing he'd been keeping from him.

"Alfred, old boy, I hear that you will be publishing a book of poetry by someone named Claude McKay? Well, you've outdone yourself this time, not only is this chap unknown but he must be a figment of your imagination because I've been checking around and no one has even heard of him."

Alfred gave his cigar a confident thump and the short ash flittered into the ashtray. His eyes were soupy when he looked at Horace; he smiled wryly and said, "That's because he's a Negro."

Horace's eyes stretched and then narrowed. He wagged his finger at Alfred and laughed. "You are a card, Alfred, a real card!"

Mainstream houses did not publish Negroes because most Negroes were illiterate and so who would buy the books? It would be a waste of ink and paper.

"I'm not pulling your leg, Horace, I'm serious."

Horace stopped laughing and looked deep into Alfred's face and saw the most earnest of expressions resting there.

"My God, you are serious," he gasped.

Alfred nodded his head.

"Well, why in the world—"

"It's magnificent, that's why."

Horace had never heard the word *magnificent* used to describe a Negro or his work. He was intrigued.

"Is that so?"

"It is."

"And how did you come by this . . . *magnificent* work? Did the chap query you directly?"

Alfred grinned, turned on his heels, and tilted his chin toward a cluster of people engaged in conversation.

"Waldo brought the manuscript in to me himself."

Horace smirked. He did not much like Waldo Frank, not the man nor the books he'd written. His feelings for Waldo were public knowledge, which was probably why Waldo was overly critical in his reviews of the books Horace published as well as the stage plays he produced.

Horace invited Waldo to his parties because it was good business to do so, but he avoided him lest he find himself on the receiving end of yet another one of Waldo's rants about the joys of mysticism.

Waldo glanced over, saw Horace staring, and raised his glass in salute.

Claude McKay's *Harlem Shadows* went on to be published to critical, commercial, and financial success, and overnight, poetry and literature written by Negroes were suddenly in demand by the white elite.

Horace was a man who knew how to feed a need, and as Alfred patiently waited for McKay to finish his first novel, Horace quietly contacted the editors at *The Crisis* and *Negro World*, advising them that he was looking for Negro writers. Within days, his office was flooded with manuscripts. He would eventually publish Jean Toomer's *Cane* and Jesse Fauset's *There Is Confusion*.

The successful real estate tycoon William Harmon, a longtime admirer of the Negro and his art, created a foundation that recognized the best in Negro artistic achievements, awarding gold, bronze, and silver medals.

Publisher J.B. Lippincott jumped on the black bandwagon and offered a $1,000 cash advance and publication for the best novel written on Negro life by a Negro. Horace, not to be outdone, implemented a similar competition, but doubled the cash prize and opened it to both Negroes and whites.

CHAPTER 27

Meredith was sitting in the parlor reading the paper when she came across the full-page announcement about the writing competition and her immediate thought was that Easter's novel would be the perfect candidate. Not the one Easter had been showing her, but the one she kept hidden under the bed in the confines of her suitcase. The one Meredith had been secretly reading. The one that Easter had yet to reveal even existed.

Every few days Easter would bring a stack of papers to Meredith for her review and Meredith would scan the pages for the loveliness, but it wasn't there and she'd go stiff with anger and ask, "Is this all you've been working on? Is there nothing else?"

And Easter would innocently bat her eyes and shake her head no.

Liar!

The more Meredith thought about it, the more she realized that Easter was playing her for a fool. Living in her apartment, eating her food, and taking her money with every intention of publishing that manuscript behind her back.

Maybe her plan was to publish it under a pseudonym, with the hope that Meredith would never be the wiser. If Easter thought that she was sorely mistaken, because Meredith Tomas would read every book ever published from that moment forward, until she found it, and when she did she would slap Easter across her face and then spit on her!

When the butler walked into the room, Meredith's face was flushed, her hands were clenched into tight fists, and she was shaking like the last leaf in autumn—she looked like she was in the throes of a stroke.

The beginning of the end looked like a brand-new day for Easter. It was as clear and encouraging as a Sunday sermon. Everyone was talking about the competition, those inside and outside of Harlem. W.E.B. DuBois, the great Negro leader and author, after hearing about it, was quoted as saying, "There is in this world no such force as the force of a person determined to rise. The human soul cannot be permanently chained, and here now is the proof!"

Horace assembled a panel of judges which included William E. Harmon, the educator and writer Brander Matthews, and the English novelist W. L. George.

The winner would be announced at the Boni & Liveright offices on April 1, the day of fools.

Just four days before the announcement, winter puckered its rime lips and blew thirteen inches of snow across the city. Schools were closed and squealing children layered in wool coats streamed from brownstones and tenement buildings out into the bright whiteness. Snow angels were made, snowmen carefully constructed, and snowballs pelted at anything that moved. By noon, though, the sun was sitting bright and high in the sky, the temperature had climbed, and the icicles began to fall. Blankets of snow liquefied and receded into the sewers and standpipes. The sound of rushing water reverberated through the city, augmenting the irritation of the men who'd gathered in the conference room at the Boni & Liveright offices. The three judges leaned back in their chairs and gazed down at two manuscripts.

Harmon said, "This is a problem."

"A big one," said George. "Plagiarism is a sin that should be punishable by law."

Matthews scratched his chin. "That might be taking it a bit far."

"I don't think so. Plagiarism is theft. In less civilized countries they cut your hand off for stealing."

"Are you calling America a civilized country?" George chuckled and the rest joined in.

Harmon raised his hands and quieted the men. "They live together, you know."

"Yes, I heard that."

"That makes this all the more difficult."

"Yes, it does."

"Well, do you think Meredith Tomas actually wrote it? I mean, we're looking for the best story written on Negro life," Matthews said.

"Are you suggesting that as a white woman she could not have written this story?" George's eyes narrowed.

"What I'm saying is that the experiences found in this story," Matthews reached over and tapped his finger against the stack of typed papers, "are much too authentic and the dialect is . . my God, dead on! I just can't imagine Meredith Tomas writing with this much precision."

George raised a finger. "I think we are disregarding the mystery of the art and the artist."

"How so?" Matthews asked.

"Let us not forget the case of Thomas Chatterton."

The men nodded agreeably. Thomas Chatterton had been writing faux medieval poetry ever since he was twelve years old and in 1769 successfully touted his poems as unearthed authentic period pieces of a fifteenth-century monk.

"Practice makes perfect, gentlemen," George said. "And let's not forget Al Jolsen."

Harmon was horrified. "What are you trying to say?"

"Jolsen, a white man, put on blackface, sang mammy, and for a few hours became a very believable Negro."

"So?"

"I think he's saying that some people are talentless save for the fact that they are excellent mimics," Matthews interjected.

"So in this case who would be the mimic?" Harmon asked.

"Why, Meredith, of course. But," George drummed his fingers thoughtfully on the oak table, "E.V. Gibbs has only written short stories, and clearly this novel was a massive undertaking, and to write a perfect novel the first time out of the gate is rare."

Harmon shook his head. "How do you know that this is her first attempt at a novel? Writers die all the time, leaving behind volumes of unpublished and unseen work!"

"You have a point."

"This novel goes far above mimicry."

"I think you are biased, Mr. Harmon."

"I don't care. Think what you want."

"Let's not bicker. We're going to have to make a decision," Matthews said.

Harmon raised his hand. "My vote is for E.V. Gibbs."

"I'm for Meredith Tomas," said George.

"I'm torn," Matthews shamefully admitted.

George dug into his pocket and pulled out a quarter. "Then I guess we'll have your Lady Liberty decide—"

"Wait, will we tell them?"

"Tell who?"

"The women . . . the writers. Gibbs and Tomas?"

"Yes, of course, I suppose we would have to."

"And the newspapers?"

"What of them?"

"Will they be notified?"

"I don't see how it can be avoided."

The men were quiet for a moment. The sounds of metal shovels scraping against the snow echoed up from the streets.

"All agreed?"

"Ay!"

"Okay then, heads, Meredith Tomas; tales, E.V. Gibbs . . ." George flicked his thumb and the coin rocketed into the air.

BOOK IV
APERTURE

CHAPTER 28

Waycross, Georgia
1961

The quarter dropped down into the brown palm of the teenage boy, who then slapped it loudly onto the back of his free hand. "Tails!" he shouted. "You have to carry the watermelon." The younger boy glumly bent over and hoisted the ten-pound melon up onto his shoulder and the two started down the dusty road. The air that day was still and the heat, heavy and damp like a black woman's working hand. It pressed against faces, armpits, scalps, and even private places, springing salty streams of water.

There were few trees on that last stretch of road, so there were only small bits of shade along the street—no defense at all against the rays of sunlight that crept under the awning of the bus station like a thief. The heat was worse inside the depot and the whirling fans just shifted it from one corner to the next, leaving Dodd Everson's face pinched and pink and finally forcing him to roll his shirtsleeves up to his elbows. When he glanced at his watch it told him that the bus was still late and his patience began to peel away.

Five minutes later the sound of a diesel engine brought a sigh of relief from Dodd and the others who were waiting for loved ones. He rolled his sleeves down again, buttoned the cuffs, and adjusted the white straw Panama hat he wore. The woman he waited for sat slumped sideways in the stiff bus seat with her cheek pressed against the window. She was asleep and her mouth was slightly ajar; a stream of saliva inched its way down her chin. The bus hit a bump in the road and jolted her awake. Her eyelids fluttered open in time to see the rusted aluminum sign on the side of the road which stated: *Ice-cold Coca-Cola served here.*

Stomach grumbling, she wiped at her chin, then began the arduous task of bringing her old body erect again. Flicking her tongue against the roof of her mouth, she unsnapped the silver clasp of the beaten black leather purse she'd clutched on her lap through four states and fished out a peppermint ball she'd been saving for just this moment.

Welcome to Waycross—population 1,856, a small wooden sign three feet from the road proclaimed. The woman rolled her eyes and snorted loudly at the black letters.

When the bus came to a shuddering stop, passengers leapt from their seats and grabbed the hatboxes, valises, and paper bags that had made the journey on the steel racks above their heads. But she was too old, too tired, and too wide to immediately tackle that particular task and so she remained in her seat.

The soldier boy who'd helped her onto the bus in Charleston and then taken the seat beside her had talked about everything, including his pretty, hazel-eyed wife waiting for him in Waycross. An hour had passed before he realized that he hadn't offered his name.

"Joseph Gill. But my friends call me Josey." Grinning, he extended a strong dark hand.

"Pleased to meet you, Josey. Easter Bartlett."

They shook.

"Pleased, Mizz Bartlett," Josey said, and then, "'Scuse me, ma'am, uhm, did you say Easter?"

"Sure did."

"Why that's certainly a unique name."

Easter nodded and mused on how the word "unique" rolled off his Southern tongue.

"Yes, that's what they tell me."

Now he was hovering over her, staring down at the dark oily spots on her battered straw hat.

"This here is Waycross, ma'am."

Easter smiled and nodded her head in agreement. She looked out the window and then back at him.

"Didn't you say you was getting off here?"

"Uh-huh, just want to take my time."

Josey heard the fatigue in Easter's voice. It was a familiar sound—as commonplace in black women as fish were to the sea.

"Of course," Josey said, and shot an anxious look outside the window.

Easter followed his eyes. "You see her?"

"Uhm, not yet."

"She'll be here. Don't look so worried." Easter began to lift her body from the seat.

"There she is!" Josey yelped. He stretched over Easter and knocked frantically on the window. "Carol!"

Easter smiled at his excitement and then tapped him gently on the waist.

"Sorry, ma'am." Josey gave her a shameful look. "Can I help you up?"

"Sure can," Easter said, taking his waiting hand. "Go easy now."

He gently pulled and she gently pushed and together they got her old body upright.

"You okay?"

"Fine, just ancient," Easter laughed. "Hand me that suitcase up there, would you?"

Off the bus, the heat wrapped itself tight around Easter as she made her way to the small depot. Josey offered to carry her suitcase, but Easter declined, sending him away with a wave of her hand. "Go on now, don't be bothering yourself with this old woman. You got babies to make!" she cackled happily.

Easter lumbered toward what she hoped would be some sort of cool—some sort of cool, and the promise of an ice-cold Coca-Cola. Her mouth began to water, turning the mint into a lump of sticky sugar on the center of her tongue. Sweat ran down her face and into her eyes, transforming Dodd Everson into a white and pink blur as he stood waiting just outside the entrance.

"Easter Bartlett?"

She looked up into his ice-blue eyes.

"Yessuh, that would be me."

CHAPTER 29

He didn't carry her bag. Didn't even offer, just introduced himself and turned on his heels and started toward a white Cadillac with a ragtop and spiked chrome wheels. There was a Confederate flag sticker on the bumper. No words, just the flag. Easter supposed that said it all.

They climbed in, Dobbs shoved the key in the ignition, and they were off. The tires cut through the dry earth, raising curtains of red dust that settled in sheets on the windshield and hood of the car. Dodd cussed under his breath and pressed down heavily on the gas pedal.

Easter clung to the armrest; he was driving too fast and her seat was too far up, pressing her belly against the dashboard. A sudden stop and she was sure she would be thrown through the windshield to her death. The thought churned her already sour stomach. A Coca-Cola would have helped with that problem, but when Easter stopped to wipe the sweat from her eyes she saw the frown on Dodd's face, and she knew that he would not allow her the time it would take to buy the Coke, just his "Is this all you got?" and her "Yessuh, this is it."

And so when the bubble of air found its way into her mouth, she parted her lips and released the loud, stinking foulness and did not follow it up with an apology.

Dodd made a face and rolled down his window and asked if Easter wouldn't mind doing the same.

They whizzed by ramshackle clapboard houses that gave way to ramblers, raised ranches, and Queen Anne Victorians. Once he came upon the street known as Vesey, he eased off the gas and they crept past the bright yellow heads of sunflowers that hung glum on their green stems, laughing children splashing happily in kidney-shaped pools, and husbands proudly pushing their brand-new Flymo lawnmowers across jade-colored lawns.

The home of Dodd and Shannon Everson was a modest blue and white bi-level with a circular porch and an attached garage. A magnolia tree sat in the front yard, its blooms covered the front walk in a blanket of pink petals.

Dodd climbed from the car, went to the trunk, and retrieved Easter's suitcase. As Easter sat fumbling with the lock, the front door was flung open and Shannon rushed squealing from the house. "Oh, Easter!"

She ran to Easter and threw her arms around her neck and Easter found herself veiled in Adorn hairspray, perfume, and gin.

"Welcome to our home, Easter. It's been so many years. It's so nice to finally see you again." Shannon beamed and planted her hands on Easter's shoulders.

Shannon was a twelve-year-old tomboy the first time she came to spend the summer at the Maryland farm with her Aunt Hazeline and her family. Back then Easter was the cook, the housekeeper, and the nanny, and Hazeline had taken to referring to her as the *all-around-everything*, because Easter was efficient at everything she did. Shannon arrived that first summer with skinned knees and her blond hair pulled back into two ponytails. She abhorred dolls and playing dress-up and preferred instead to climb trees and capture frogs with her male cousins.

Shannon spent four consecutive summers at the farm. Each year she arrived with one less boyish trait, until finally she transformed into the young woman her parents had prayed for. Shannon had never forgotten Easter and so by the time Shannon sent the letter asking if she would come to Waycross to be the *all-around-everything* to her family, Easter was grateful because she had spent three years watching the cancer run like a freight train through Hazeline's body until it made its final stop in her brain.

Waycross was not a place Easter wanted to return to, but she had no other options for employment and over the years she had made her peace with the town and so she sent word back to Shannon, agreeing to come.

"Nice to see you again, Miss Shannon," Easter said when Shannon finally broke the embrace.

"You put on some weight, I see," Shannon laughed.

"That comes with age, I guess."

"I suppose it happens to the best of us," Shannon said wistfully and slid her hands down her slim hips. "C'mon in the house, you must be hungry from that long ride."

Inside was inviting and filled with sunlight. A pink and white vase regurgitating a rainbow of flowers sat on the sofa table. The living room led to the family room, which looked into the backyard. The dining room was separated from the kitchen by a swinging door.

"You sit yourself right down," Shannon gushed, and pulled a chair from beneath the round, white kitchen table. "We have some leftover pot roast, julienne carrots, and mashed potatoes." Shannon tilted the oven door open, reached in, and pulled out a casserole dish. "I've been keeping it warm for you."

A bluebird fluttered to the window, peered in, and then fluttered away. Easter supposed that this was a good sign. She was smiling to herself when Shannon paused, looked over her shoulder, and said, "Oh, it's going to be so good to have you here. I can hardly wait for the children to meet you." Shannon set the plate of food down before Easter. "They're just going to love you."

Easter opened her mouth to speak but Shannon continued, "Now, what can I get you to drink? We got sweet tea and Coca-Cola. Oh, and I think there's some ginger ale and—"

"Ma'am?"

Shannon stumbled to a stop. Her eyebrows rose in surprise, her lips parted.

"I'd like to freshen up a bit, if you don't mind."

Shannon's eyes rolled in her head and she went pink. "Oh, silly me, just going on and on. Of course you can, let me just show you where."

A small room off the kitchen between the laundry room and the pantry, a room not even big enough for a child but crammed with a bed, bureau, nightstand, and what looked to Easter like a kneeling bench. The walls were a bland peach.

"This is the closet." Shannon pointed a finger at the door on the left side of the room and then nodded to the right and said, "That's the bathroom."

"Thank you."

The bathroom, with its blue and white flowered tile, had a pleasant feel about it. A small potted cactus sat on the windowsill. Easter washed her hands, threw water onto her face, and rinsed her mouth clean. When she returned to the kitchen Shannon was seated on the counter, her legs crossed at the knee, laughing gaily on the phone. ·

CHAPTER 30

The front door opened and then closed.

A voice incredibly similar to Shannon's rang shrill through the house. "Mother!"

Easter was aproned and seated at the kitchen table skinning cucumbers while she tried to remember just how it was Dodd Everson said he preferred his steak.

"Mother!"

The kitchen door swung violently open.

"MOTHER!"

Easter's eyes met the angry ones of Alice Everson, the twelve-year-old daughter.

"Oh," Alice breathed.

"Afternoon, miss."

Alice considered Easter for a moment before sauntering over to the refrigerator and retrieving a pop. She circled the older woman like a curious cat. Easter didn't raise her eyes. After a while Alice leaned a scrawny hipbone into the edge of the table and said, "So, you must be the new girl."

Easter didn't answer.

Alice cocked her head to one side, licked her young lips. "You deaf or something?"

"No."

"You got a name?"

Girl.

"Uh-hmmm."

Alice waited, but Easter offered nothing more than the quick movement of the knife against the green of the cucumber. Irritated, Alice slammed the bottle on the table and then folded her arms across her chest.

"Well, are you going to tell me your name or not?"

"My name is Easter Bartlett."

Alice smirked and said, "Strange name for a colored woman." And then turned and walked out of the kitchen, leaving the half-empty bottle of soda.

"Strange name for a strange life," Easter mumbled to the emptiness.

She met the boy next. He was a dull-eyed, short, stocky ten-year-old thumb-sucker.

"Easter, this is Junior," Dobbs said in passing, as he lifted the lid of the pot and sniffed.

Junior pulled his thumb from his mouth and used it to quell an itch on his cheek. "Hi."

"Hello, Junior."

Easter was hopeful. *Maybe this one has manners*, she thought as she moved to the buffet. Behind her Junior pointed and laughed, "Wow, your behind is as big as a bull cow's!"

After the life she'd led, few things surprised her. But Junior's boorishness—so soon after the innocent greeting—took her off guard and the dinner plates rattled in her hands.

"Boy, how many times have I told you there ain't no such thing as a bull cow? It's either a bull or a cow!" Dobbs corrected.

Easter waited for chastising about the insult, but it never came.

* * *

Time is a tireless bird with silver feathers and broad wings. She had written that line when she was living at 409 Edgecombe Avenue and now it floated to her as she sat on the edge of her bed staring at the peach walls.

She'd put highways, big cities, years, seasons, tears, and once even the great Atlantic Ocean between herself and that place, but no distance, great or small, could erase the memory of it. It always seemed to be lurking about, bearing down on her like a truck with its headlights set on high beam. And it was there again, crammed into that small room, sucking out all of the air.

Uh-uh. No you don't, Easter shook her finger at the memories.

Looking for a distraction, she reached over and turned the silver knob of the television. A white dot appeared at the center of the black screen and slowly bloomed into a sheet of gray static. Easter fiddled with the antenna and ghostly figures appeared behind the blizzard, before the screen went black again.

Easter sighed, turned the television off, went into the bathroom, and shut the door. The memories complained loudly and rapped incessantly on the wood, tempting her with the tinkering sounds of piano keys, gay laughter, and the clink of champagne flutes meeting in salute.

They called to her, *Easter, come on out, girl!*

Easter hummed a spiritual over the din as she tied her white scarf over her shiny curls. Another knock and then Rain's voice, *Easter, you okay in there, honey?*

She dropped the toilet seat, sat down on the lid, squeezed her eyes shut, and stopped her ears with her fingers.

CHAPTER 31

She was pushing a dust rag across the sofa table when Shannon said, "I'm having some of the ladies over today for lunch."

"Yessum."

"Could you whip up some of that potato salad you make so well?"

"Yessum."

"Oh, and those finger sandwiches and maybe a—"

"Cheese plate?"

"Yes. That is exactly what I was going to suggest. It's almost as if you have tele—tele . . ."

"Telepathy."

"That's it!" Shannon said. "You were always so smart."

Shannon offered up her warmest smile and then used the tip of a fingernail to tap the rim of the empty martini glass she held. "When you get a moment, Easter."

The women arrived in twos until they totaled a dozen. Brown, blond, and red-haired, rouged cheeks and short skirts, their three-inch heels clicked musically against the marble floor of the entryway.

They talked PTA, politics, and war. The third round of drinks left them slumped in their seats, as they laughed and waded their way through gutters of gossip.

"You see that new manager at the Piggly Wiggly? If I was just ten years younger!"

"I wouldn't have married that sorry-ass husband of mine, that's for sure."

Shannon wobbled over to the console and peered down into the nearly empty ice bucket. "You know, I was crowned Miss Cornflower," she slurred.

The women exchanged knowing looks and waited for what always came.

"I could have gone onto the state competition, but Mama got ill and, well . . ."

The women sat up straight in their chairs and began to examine their watches, powder their noses, and pat strands of stiff hair back into place.

"Papa said the entry fee had to go for Mama's medicine and I was stuck. Stuck in this dust bowl of a town, playing nursemaid to my mother. Emptying sick pans and . . ."

Black mascara streaked down her cheeks. The women shifted uncomfortably. They looked to one another, their eyes asking, *Whose turn is it this time?*

The tall, lanky one with the Marilyn Monroe mole rose from her chair and walked over to the weeping Shannon.

"Now honey, you did just fine," she cooed and wrapped her arms around Shannon's trembling shoulders. "You married a wonderful man. And look at this house! It's just beautiful, yes it is. You've done real good for yourself, honey, real good."

"I guess," Shannon sniffed.

"Two wonderful kids, a nice comfortable home, a hard-working husband. What else could you want?"

Out, Shannon thought. *I want out.*

Later, when the sky turned gray and the summer rain patted softly at the windows, Easter helped a drunk Shannon up to her bedroom, where she undressed her and put her to bed. She went to the window and gazed out at the gloomy day and was reminded of a day in Harlem, a day just like this when a dark-skinned boy with slanted eyes and slick black hair showed up at the door, dripping wet. The butler made him wait in the hallway. Rain was asleep, so Meredith called Easter into her room, pressed two folded bills into her hand, and asked her to retrieve the package from the boy.

What did she know?

She handed him the money and the boy handed her the soggy brown paper bag. Easter assumed it was food, but the bag was as light as a feather and when she removed the red paper container and unfolded the flaps, what she found inside was not chop suey or fried rice, but a gold-colored powder Easter had never seen before.

What she began to notice was that each time the slanted-eyed boy showed up, Meredith's behavior became erratic; her slights against Rain grew more toxic, often escalating to hurtful and humiliating degrees. She called Rain names: "You yellow bitch!" "You swamp nigger!" Sometimes she spat at her. And Rain did nothing in return.

After a few days, Meredith's nastiness would retreat into the cave from which it came, replaced by the syrupy-sweet Meredith—the sickening, saccharine alter ego who swooned, coddled, fawned, and gifted.

Meredith never turned her ugliness on Easter, even

though it was clear she wanted to. Easter could see it in her eyes, sizzling like hot stones. Sometimes she'd look up to find Meredith glaring at her with bared teeth. But when their eyes met, the fierceness in Meredith's face disintegrated and she would grin sheepishly, like a child caught with her hand in the cookie jar. And then one Tuesday the apartment was thrust into a perpetual state of darkness when Meredith took the red container to her bedroom, only to reemerge hours later and order the butler to paint all of the windows black.

CHAPTER 32

Alice hadn't said more than a few sentences to Easter since the day she arrived. But she'd been watching her, making sure she didn't carry away the good silverware or the Fabergé egg that Shannon said she would sell when the time came for Alice to go off to college. Alice watched her the way she'd watched all of the other maids they'd had because her father said most coloreds were liars and thieves. They couldn't help it, it was hereditary, like the color of their skin and the coarseness of their hair. And they were stupid too. Good for fieldwork, housework, shucking and jiving, but little else.

And Alice had believed him, until she heard the colored man named King speaking on the radio about civil rights for Negroes. At the sound of his voice the hairs on Alice's arms had stood at attention. She had been surprised at her reaction and looked shamefully around to see if her parents had noticed.

There was a doctor on the colored side of town, but he wasn't on the radio and he hadn't met with President Kennedy. So what made this Dr. King so special?

"Mama?"

"Yes?"

"What kind of doctor is Dr. Martin Luther King?"

Shannon shrugged her shoulders and walked off to another part of the house.

Dobbs cut the radio off and said, "Probably not a doctor at all, just a title he gave himself so's he could sound important." And then he marched off muttering, "Niggers gonna turn the whole country to shit."

"Yeah, to shit!" Junior concurred.

Easter sat in the rocking chair on the porch, her black felt hat with the crooked purple flower propped awkwardly on her head. She clutched in her lap a worn straw purse with a cane handle. She was tapping her foot and smoking a cigarette. It was Sunday, her one full day off.

Alice spied on her from the den window and held her nose against the stench of the tobacco, waving away the ribbons of smoke that snaked through the screen and hung like a net around her face.

Every Sunday it was the same. Easter sitting in that rocking chair, wearing that ridiculous hat, smoking and tapping her foot like there was a band playing right there on the front lawn. And not that it mattered, Alice told herself, but she did wonder why her father never offered Easter a ride to her church. There was plenty of room in the Cadillac, even though Junior was as fat as a hog. But she hardly took up any space at all, so there was plenty of room for Easter.

Alice swept her hair from her face, straightened her back, and walked toward the front door. When she stepped out onto the porch she pretended to be startled by Easter's presence. "Oh my goodness, you frightened me," Alice said in her best Grace Kelly voice.

Easter nodded her head but said nothing. If the girl was going to sneak around spying on her, Easter mused to herself, she'd better stop wearing that Topaz talcum powder she loved so much.

"Off to church?" Alice casually asked.

Easter stopped rocking, looked dramatically to her right and then to her left, where Alice stood staring, and replied, "I'm sorry, are you speaking to me?"

Alice pursed her lips, pressed her fists into her hips, and said, "Ain't nobody else out here but us, who you think I'm talking to, myself?"

Easter chuckled, "My mistake."

Alice glared at her. "Well, are you going to church or not?"

Easter mashed the cigarette into the ashtray and looked up at the sky. "Hmmm, tell the truth, I haven't decided what I'm going to do on this beautiful Sunday."

Most Sundays she went to the sanctified church, not to pray—she could do that anywhere and at any time—but to be enveloped in the language, to revel in the music, to be swept up in the rapture. Sunday service was sustenance and Easter often found her mouth agape, tongue lapping.

The church of her childhood had grown in the decades she'd been away. New wings had been added and it now sat precariously on the border of a red-light district that didn't exist when Easter was a child.

The minister welcomed everyone, sinners and Christians alike, and often proclaimed, "We are God's children—each and every one of us!"

No one in that congregation was as pure as the driven snow, but some were more soiled than others—the flesh peddlers, gamblers, parolees, drug dealers, and drug users sat up in the balcony in the Nigger Heaven section of the church, where the ceiling was so low you had to stoop to keep from hitting your head on the rafters. Easter sat up there too, she liked to think that being up high like that made it convenient for God to reach down and press his lovely index finger against her woolen head.

But on that day she didn't go to church; she walked right past it and down the road to the cemetery where she pardoned and excused herself to the dead as she sidestepped her way along the narrow dirt aisles that separated the graves. Her mother's plot was marked with a small heart-shaped headstone. Easter traced her fingers gently over the etched letters and numbers.

Zelda Marie Bartlett
1875–1910

It wasn't easy, but she managed to ease herself down onto her knees. Getting up would take some time, but time was all she had. The cemetery was on a lovely plot of land that white folks muttered would be made better use of if the bodies were relocated and it was turned into a park.

It was the only piece of land in Waycross blanketed in beautiful Kentucky bluegrass. That grass shimmered like an ocean beneath the light of the full moon and the trees that dotted that land were the oldest and largest in the area.

"So, Mama, how you been? Good? . . . Oh, that's nice to hear . . . What was that? . . . Oh, the Eversons are fine, just fine. You know, typical white folks stuff. What you gonna do? You gotta laugh to keep from crying, right? You the one that taught me that."

Easter patted the dirt affectionately.

"Pardon?" She turned her head, eyed the fields across the road. "No, I haven't," she whispered, then picked up a pebble and tossed it aside. "You know I don't write stories anymore," she said dryly.

Alice thought herself sly—she claimed a stomachache, and to authenticate the claim she made sure her mother heard her retching in the bathroom. Shannon made her some tea, placed a few saltines on a napkin, and set it on the nightstand by Alice's bed.

As soon as the Cadillac pulled out of the driveway, Alice was up and out the back door, running like the wind toward the colored side of town.

Alice thought herself invisible, but still kept a safe distance, following Easter like a shadow and then hiding behind the tree as Easter conversed with the dead.

She may have been able to fool her parents, but Easter was wise to her, because she had caught the scent of Topaz talcum powder in the air.

CHAPTER 33

Easter saw that Shannon hardly paid any attention to Alice—not the way you think a woman with only two children and no job could.

The longing in Alice's eyes was painful and could have been easily mitigated with a hug, and not just the gratuitous kind that Shannon offered in reward for a gold-starred report or an A on a math test. Easter's mother had hugged her children often—"just because" hugs were the best ones of all. Shannon's interaction with her children swung between terror and aversion.

So on the evening when Alice spat up Easter's creamy mashed potatoes, green beans, and broiled steak, Shannon's face curled in disgust and she assisted her daughter at arm's length. She managed to remove Alice's clothes and put her into bed without getting any of the puke on herself. After that she bid her children goodbye and she and Dobbs climbed into the Cadillac and hightailed it across town where they were due to attend a garden party.

So it was Easter, not Shannon, who knocked softly on Alice's door and asked just as quietly if it was all right if she came in. And it was Easter who filled the tub with warm water and then said, "Come on in here," with motherly authority. "Temperature just right and I put some of that bubble bath in there that you like."

Alice walked into the bathroom wrapped in a yellow flannel robe with pockets shaped like ducks. Easter reached for the knotted belt of the robe and Alice shrank back.

"Miss Alice, believe me, I have seen it all."

Alice remained steadfast. "Turn around."

Easter smirked and did as she was told and Alice quickly shirked the robe off, stepped out of her underwear, and leapt into the tub.

"Okay, you can turn around now," Alice said after she was sure every inch of her was hidden beneath the bubbles.

"You want me to wash your back?"

Alice thought about it for a moment. She couldn't remember her own mother ever making that offer. She shrugged her shoulders, shifted her eyes, and began to pick at the grout between the tiles.

Easter gently pulled the washcloth across Alice's back. The stiffness in the girl's body gradually melted away and the tendons in her neck went slack. She scratched her nose and chanced a glance at Easter and saw that she was lost in thought, staring at the floor.

"What?" Alice asked as she peered over the edge of the tub.

"Umpf," Easter sounded. She dropped the cloth into the water, dried her hands on her skirt, and bent to retrieve what she'd been staring at. "So this is the problem."

Alice looked at her underwear and blinked. "What is it?"

Easter brought the undergarment closer and Alice saw that there was a streak of pink in the seat. Her eyes ballooned with fright. "Is that . . . blood?" she asked in a quivering voice.

Easter nodded her head.

Alice recalled a neighbor who suddenly began to experience nosebleeds. Three months later she had a brain tumor. Two weeks after that she was dead.

Alice's breath came in short pants. "Am I . . . Am I dying!" she wailed.

Easter was taken aback by the child's reaction and placed a settling hand on her shoulder. "No, baby, you're not dying, you're becoming a woman."

Alice gave Easter a blank look.

"Didn't your mother tell you about this?"

Alice shook her head no.

"She never told you about your monthly friend?"

Alice had heard her mother and her mother's friends use that phrase, but she sincerely thought it was a real, live female friend.

Easter tossed the soiled underwear into the sink, took a deep breath, and began to explain to Alice what Shannon had failed to.

After the bath, the two sat on the end of the bed with their thighs slightly touching.

"So every month?"

Easter nodded her head. "Every single month."

"Every month until I die?"

Easter laughed, "Well, not quite that long."

Alice fiddled with the balls of lint on her pajama bottoms. "Do you still . . . ?"

"Nope." Easter's response was curt. "C'mon now, it's late, your mother will have my hide if she comes home to find that you're still up. C'mon now, under the covers."

Alice allowed Easter to tuck her in. What followed was normal and natural, but still left the two of them breathless with astonishment.

Alice threw her hands around Easter's neck and pressed a kiss into her brown cheek.

CHAPTER 34

Miss Anthony, Alice's squirrelly, bifocaled seventh-grade teacher, clapped her hands together and ordered her students to be quiet. She was grinning so hard her face looked as if it would crack. "Children," she sang, "today is a very exciting day." She came from behind the desk. "Today the library has received a very special gift."

"A horse?" Abigail Sessions shouted excitedly.

Miss Anthony's face fell slack. "No, not a horse," she said as she waved the ridiculous statement away. "Today the library received the personal papers of a very well-respected and celebrated author named Meredith Tomas."

Delia Eubanks, who often bragged that she was the best reader in the world because her mother, Lollie Eubanks, was the town librarian, stated in a condescending tone, "Meredith Tomas? Well, I've never heard of her."

"Have we forgotten that we must be called on if we want to speak?" Miss Anthony's tone was cutting, but sweet. "And Delia, I'm sure that there are many, many writers you are not familiar with."

A chuckle rippled through the classroom.

"Meredith Tomas was a recipient of the Rosenfeld and Guggenheim—two very important and distinguished honors. She published poetry in her early years, then a number of short stories and novels later on in life. Her most famous novel, *Sentiments in the Eves*, is her greatest, most celebrated work."

The students looked bored.

"And do you know why we should be proud of that?"

The students shook their heads.

"Because the story takes place right here in Waycross, that's why!"

The children reacted indifferently, but Miss Anthony was not to be deflated.

"In fact, the *New York Times* called it the greatest work ever written on Negro life by a non-Negro!" She clapped her hands excitedly.

Abigail's hand shot up in the air and began waving like a flag. Miss Anthony nodded in her direction.

"Too bad the coloreds won't be able to read the book."

Miss Anthony's eyelids fluttered and she reached for the fake pearls around her neck. "And why is that?"

"Cause the library don't grant coloreds library cards, that's why," said Abigail pointedly.

Miss Anthony went red. "Oh, oh yes. I forgot," she whispered.

"And anyway," a burly boy named Elijah interjected, "coloreds don't read no how."

"Well, now—" Miss Anthony started, but Alice jumped to her feet and shouted, "Yes they do too! My maid reads!"

Easter was making chicken soup with dumplings, diced

carrots, and potatoes that she'd taken the time to cut into perfect cubes. When she reached for the ladle, she caught sight of a young Easter peering at her from the silver belly of the utensil. Gleaming marcelled hair, thin eyebrows, and a face painted like Clara Bow. She would never have gone out into streets looking like that. Well, the marcelled hair was fine, but the whorish makeup? Never!

But up at 409 Edgecombe every day was Halloween. Meredith had the windows blacked out and then she draped Rain's scarves and boas over everything with a limb—chandeliers, doorknobs, and vacant picture hooks. She insisted that they live by candlelight and candlelight alone. Guests were only received if they arrived wearing Venetian masks.

The three of them lived like unaccompanied minors, spending their days playing dress-up, walking on the furniture, eating pancakes for dinner, roast beef for breakfast, and cake for supper. They filled the bathtub with three cases of champagne, jumped in, and splashed about like seals. And through it all, the little slanted-eyed boy came and went.

It was sweet delirium for weeks, and then after that it was just delirium.

"Easter, Easter!"

Easter remained hushed in her memories.

The backdoor creaked open and Shannon stumbled in. "Easter, what in the world is wrong with you? I've been calling you since forever!"

"Ma'am?"

Shannon shot Easter an annoyed look. "I said," she began slowly, "I've been calling you for some time."

Easter rested the ladle down on the table and wiped at her eyes. "Sorry, just lost in my work, I guess."

"Really?" Shannon spouted sarcastically.

Easter reached for the bottle of BMX.

"I want a bologna sandwich, not too much mayonnaise and no lettuce," Shannon said as she stroked her neck. "And another martini."

Easter nodded. It was 1:30.

It was just as well because she hadn't wanted to keep thinking about that time.

CHAPTER 35

Easter was having a good laugh out there in the garden all by herself. Alice bit into an apple and watched curiously from the opposite side of the mesh screen. She was drawn to her now. She offered her help around the house, asked Easter to teach her how to snap the dust rag the way she'd seen her do. When Easter wasn't looking, Alice stole her Pall Malls and hid behind the garage and practiced blowing smoky circles into the air.

She questioned Easter about Dr. King's credentials and Easter was more than happy to enlighten her. And the question Alice posed about Negroes having tails almost broke Easter in two with laughter as she assured her that she had never met anyone with a tail.

Alice crept outside, careful not to let the door slam, and when Easter turned around the girl was less than two feet away from her.

"What you want, child?" Easter asked, panting. "Ain't proper to be sneaking up on an old woman like that. Could give me a heart attack and then who would cook your meals and wash your dirty drawers!" Her tone was filled with humor and her eyes shimmered wet with joyful tears.

"What's so funny?"

"This." Easter leaned over, bent her knees, crossed

her eyes, and stuck her tongue out of the corner of her mouth. She raised herself up onto the balls of her feet, planted both hands on her kneecaps, and proceeded to flap her legs together like wings. It was the most ridiculous dance Alice had ever seen.

"What are you doing that for?"

"Just being silly, sometimes you have to just be silly!"

Alice was afraid for her. She felt a woman her size and her age shouldn't be exerting herself in that fashion. "Stop it," she whispered fearfully, but Easter ignored her.

"Come on, you try it."

Alice folded her arms. "Nope. And you shouldn't be doing it either, it makes you look ridiculous."

"Aw, c'mon," Easter pleaded between laughs.

The stupid dance and the joy that Easter seemed to derive from it were infectious and Alice found the corners of her mouth twitching. A giggle tickled its way up her throat and then burst from her mouth in a snort, causing Easter to howl. Alice acquiesced—she crossed her eyes and began imitating Easter's outrageous movements. They laughed and danced until they were so tired they could do little more than collapse into the patio chairs.

"Where did you learn to do that?"

Easter tilted her head toward the blue sky. "Ah," she breathed, "a very long time ago in a place far, far away."

While the children were asleep and Dobbs and Shannon Everson sat on opposite ends of the sofa watching *The Dean Martin Show*, Easter was out on the porch in the rocking chair, listening to crickets hum as she read the newspaper by moonlight.

She read articles about a rogue hog, socialism in Cuba, the suicide of Ernest Hemingway, and the impending arrival of the personal papers donated to the town's library by the now deceased, renowned writer Meredith Tomas.

Her mind had been known to play tricks on her and so to be sure, Easter reread the lines and then smoked four cigarettes, in succession, down to the butts. When she went to bed that night, her mind was a tornado of images that swept her back to the moment that became her first step in a long journey back to the very place she had run away from.

CHAPTER 36

In Harlem the streets burned with gossip. Apparently the penthouse at 409 Edgecombe, which Meredith had playfully dubbed Heaven, had turned into some type of hell.

Meredith was no longer taking visitors—no matter how extraordinarily beautiful their Venetian masks were. The phone rang without answer until the line went dead. The grocery store had not delivered food to the penthouse in weeks. Someone had suggested that the Negro women who lived there had mutinied and tied Meredith to the wooden post of her bed and were forcing her to eat out of her dog's bowl. If the butler wasn't dead, said the concerned individual, then he was in on it too. "We can't waste any more time. Something has to be done, I'm going to call the authorities."

When the butler answered the door, the police officers' rigid stance immediately relaxed. They asked for Meredith Tomas and a look of disdain wafted across the butler's face. He ushered them into the music room where he instructed them to wait. Minutes later, Meredith floated in draped in golden silk pajamas; her hair was covered in a matching cloche.

She batted heavy lashes at them and purred, "How can I help you today, officers?"

They stated the concerns of the worried acquaintance and as they did their eyes crawled over her, expertly examining her body for bruises, her eyes for fear or insanity, and felt like idiots when they found nothing.

Meredith laughed, "Do I look like a woman in peril?" And she took the hand of the more handsome officer and started toward the parlor where Easter and Rain were lounging on the sofa with playing cards in their hands. They raised their eyes when Meredith and the officers entered and Easter uttered, "Oh, hello," and Rain said, "Never mind them, go fish."

In the hallway, as the officers stood waiting for the elevator, they fathomed that they had been made the butt of someone's lame joke. Nothing at all looked out of place in that apartment; it was *odd* that the windows were blacked out, but other than that, nothing. Normal.

The handsome officer stomped his police force–issued boot and slapped his thigh. "Hey, I forgot, it's April first!"

"So?"

"April first, April Fool's Day."

"Oh yeah. Well, they got us good."

When the elevator doors slid open a young boy dressed in gray knickers and matching jacket stepped out. The gold tin badge pinned to the front of the hat he wore read, *Western Union*.

The boy snapped his hand to his forehead in salute and the officers returned the gesture and then stepped laughing into the elevator.

Most mornings Easter hummed, or at the very least muttered to herself in a singsong fashion. But her night had been filled with bitter memories that left a ball of anger in her throat, and so she was as quiet as a leaf while she prepared and served the family breakfast. Dobbs opened his mouth to make a request, but Easter slammed the platter of pancakes down so hard onto the table that his mouth snapped shut again.

There was no conversation that morning. Even Junior was quiet. In the kitchen Easter cussed under her breath, banged pots together, and dumped a whole tray of silverware into the sink. The family exchanged nervous glances and then one-by-one disappeared to different parts of the house. Only Alice remained at the table, and when the door swung open again, Easter charged into the dining room like a wild boar and began clearing the table.

"Um, Easter, I—"

Easter stopped, raised her head, and glared at Alice. "Why you always up under me, huh?"

Alice found herself blinking uncontrollably.

"Go on outside and play, go on away from me."

Easter spun around and slammed back through the door, leaving Alice seated at the table, choking on her tears.

CHAPTER 37

To Miss Anthony's dismay, Meredith's personal papers—a dozen handwritten letters, several newspaper clippings, and five first-edition, autographed copies of her debut novel, along with a few photographs of her posed with notable scribes—arrived in Waycross without even a hint of fanfare.

Miss Anthony herself transported the items from the train station to the library and arranged them under two separate glass showcases that were set on a wooden table and positioned near the entrance of the library so they couldn't be missed.

The following Monday Miss Anthony brought her class to the library to view the treasures. Hardly able to contain her excitement, she flittered about like a bird as she pointed out various articles and objects behind the glass. She spewed information—both historical and hearsay—with all the reserve of a greyhound awaiting the gunshot.

Again the children looked bored.

"Okay, boys and girls, you can go and pick your books for the week," she said, and all of the children except Alice quickly scattered. Miss Anthony was thrilled.

Alice held her face so close to the glass that her breath left little clouds of fog on the surface. The name wasn't

right: *E.V. Gibbs*. But that face—younger and thinner—
was definitely Easter's. She was sure of it.

The *Tattler* article read:

> *Best Novel on Negro Life Competition (April 1, 1923)*
> *Publisher Horace Liveright offered a prize of $2,000 and a*
> *publishing contract for the best novel written on Negro life.*
> *Liveright reportedly received over two hundred entries, but*
> *regrets that there is only one prize. The winning announce-*
> *ment was made today. Liveright told this reporter, "Only*
> *two of the entries proved admissible for the conditions pre-*
> *sented and those two had a remarkable number of 'literary*
> *coincidences.' The judges labored over the two entries for*
> *days and in the end decided that the rightful owner of the*
> *manuscript and the winner of the competition is novelist*
> *and Negrophile, Meredith Tomas."*
>
> *When asked who the "other" entrant was, a source,*
> *who shall remain nameless, advised that it was none other*
> *than short story writer and essayist E.V. Gibbs—who, as some*
> *of you know, is the widow of Marcus Garvey's would-be*
> *assassin and secretary to Meredith Tomas. You put two and*
> *two together. Can you say plagiarist?*

CHAPTER 38

Sunday came around again and Easter left the house just as the morning light spread across the rooftops. In those early hours, a shutting door sounded like a tree falling and Alice's eyes popped open at the sound. She thought of the silverware, the Fabergé egg, and the word "plagiarist," and wrestled with the sheets and the blanket before tumbling out of bed and rushing to the window. She caught a glimpse of the bobbing purple flower as Easter made her way down the road. A minute later, sneakers in hand, sleep crusted at the corners of her eyes, Alice snuck past the closed door of her parents' bedroom, down the stairs, and out the door.

Easter marched down the road like a soldier off to war. It was the same tread she used the day she left Waycross, then Valdosta, and, in later years, Harlem, Philly, Chicago—the list was endless. But this was the end of the line for her now. There was no place else for her to go. The doors were closed to places she hadn't been; she was just too old to start over.

And what a sorrowful ending to a life that had at times sparked and snapped with excitement. The road behind her was paved with good and bad, and that was fine—that was life. But to come to the end of one's days and find that the person who had smiled in your face while sinking a blade deep into your back, the person who had hated and despised you so severely, was now bringing you more misery even as she lay dead and cold in her coffin—well, that was just too much for any person to swallow.

Easter had refused to hate Meredith Tomas—had refused despite the fact that her life was turning to dust. She'd seen what hate could do. Her mother had said that hate was a chain that dragged you under—but Easter now feared that she was wrong because she'd seen people stand on the shoulders of hate and pluck money and power from the very top shelves of the universe.

What had not hating gotten her? A twin bed in a closet-sized room off the kitchen of her white employer's home, that's what! And what was that? That was shit!

Alice could barely keep up and stay out of sight at the same time. She'd tailed Easter past the church and deep into the colored section of the town. Alice had never been that far on foot and she felt her heart begin to clamor. "Where in the world is she going?" she wondered aloud.

Easter stopped, turned her head back and forth as if she was lost, and then abruptly started walking again. She stepped off the road and into a cornfield.

Easter violently shoved the stalks aside, clearing a straight path for Alice to follow. At the foot of the field the land spread green again, and even though the house Easter grew up in was gone, she recognized the place to be her childhood home.

The oak tree was taller than she remembered; it towered so high that when she tilted her head back to gaze at it, she became dizzy.

Alice crouched down and watched Easter circle the trunk of the tree, and then Easter grabbed hold of the tree and struggled down to her knees. From her pocketbook, she removed a spoon and began to dig. After a few moments she raised her head and used the back of her hand to wipe sweat from her forehead and the tears from her eyes.

She dug until the heap of unearthed dirt resembled a pyramid and the spoon finally hit tin.

Alice crept closer and squinted at the object Easter had unearthed, but from where she stood she couldn't quite make it out.

Easter sat back on her haunches and gently brushed the dirt from the tin, revealing the red and brown paisley design. Time and the elements had rusted the lid shut and Easter wrestled with it for quite some time, slamming it angrily against the bark of the tree, flinging it down to the ground, pounding it with her fist, but to no avail.

Frustrated and whipped, she collapsed against the tree and gazed down at her torn stockings and filthy dress. The rounded toes of Alice's sneakers suddenly stepped into view. Easter raised her eyes and was genuinely surprised to see the girl standing there.

"No talcum today, huh?"

Alice was lost. "Pardon?"

"Never mind," Easter said. "What you doing here?"

Alice couldn't speak the truth, because she didn't exactly know what the truth was, so she just shrugged her shoulders.

Easter scrutinized her for a moment and then stuck her hand out. "Well, don't just stand there doing nothing, help me up."

Once she was on her feet she brushed the dirt from her dress and righted her hat on her head. She glanced at the hole and the heap of dirt and then turned to Alice and asked, "Your parents know you out here?"

Alice shook her head no.

Easter sighed and slipped the strap of her purse over her shoulder. "Well, you followed me all of the way out here for some reason, so what is it?"

Alice mumbled something Easter couldn't hear.

"Speak up, child."

Alice fastened on Easter the most intense look she'd ever seen a child give. "Are you E.V. Gibbs?"

Easter didn't know whether to smack Alice's face or just ignore the question. In the end she looked stupidly back at the child and said, "Who's that again?"

Because she had never really known that person.

CHAPTER 39

Miss Anthony had no business in the colored section of town at the time of the morning—or any other time of the day, for that matter. But there she was doing forty down the road with the windows open and the wind in her hair. The volume on the radio was turned up and she was singing along to Ben E. King's "Stand by Me" when she spotted two figures stepping from the forest of corn. She sped past them, and recognized one of the two as her student, Alice Everson. Miss Anthony smashed her foot down on the brake so hard that the tires squealed and the car spun, screeching to a stop on the opposite side of the road, facing oncoming traffic.

She composed herself, turned the car around, and slowly coasted to the spot where Easter and Alice stood frozen and staring. She leaned over the seat and through the open window called, "Morning." Her eyes were fixed curiously on Easter. "Alice, you sure out early. Everything okay?"

Alice nodded her head and Easter said, "Everything is just fine. Just fine."

"What you all doing out here . . . so early?"

Alice stammered an excuse but Easter shoved her gently aside, bent over and rested her forearm on the metal ledge of the window, and began a slow and deliberate inspection. She looked Miss Anthony in the eye and then off in the direction she'd come from, before shifting her gaze down to the skirt Miss Anthony wore that exposed most of her thighs. Easter's eyes traveled to the woman's bare feet and then over to the high-heeled shoes that lay on the passenger seat. An unmistakable musk wafted off Miss Anthony's body; you only had to be with one black man to know that scent, and Miss Anthony reeked of it.

Easter's eyes met squarely with Miss Anthony's again and she turned the woman's inquiry on its side. "I might ask you that same question, ma'am."

Miss Anthony's face went red. She was not a stupid woman. Easter had made herself quite clear. And so she swiped the shoes off the seat, swallowed, and blurted, "Can I give you a ride?"

"Well thank you, ma'am, that is mighty nice of you," Easter smiled.

Shannon just stared at the two of them. They were quite a sight, Easter muddied from the waist down and Alice bedraggled with bits of . . . "Is that corn husk in your hair?" Any real mother would have shown some hint of interest, anger, or alarm, but Shannon's only concern lay in the glass of gin and orange juice she clutched in her hand. And so she dismissed them with an exasperated roll of her eyes.

Miss Anthony hoped she hadn't seemed rude, but something about that Negro woman was familiar and she couldn't help but stare. Their eyes had met in the rear-view mirror a number of times and she had smiled and

the woman had smiled back. Numerous times Miss Anthony wanted to ask, *Do I know you?* But the words never
came out. And now, as she readied herself for church,
the nagging, knowing feeling persisted.

CHAPTER 40

Easter had tossed the small round tin into her purse and there it remained, forgotten for the hours that fell between Sunday morning and Monday afternoon. Forgotten by Easter, but not Alice, who thought about it in the way a child thinks about Christmas or summer vacation.

She had a whole two dollars saved and offered one to Junior if he would cause a distraction that would warrant Easter's attention. He agreed, of course, being the filthy urchin that he was, and dropped to the ground and feigned a fit complete with flailing hands and feet. While he wailed, gurgled, and frothed, Alice slipped into Easter's bedroom, rummaged through her drawers, looked under the bed, and finally found the straw purse with the cane handle and the prize hidden inside and cried, "Eureka!"

With the tin tucked safely in the pocket of her denim overalls, Alice sidled up behind Easter who had jabbed the business end of the wooden spoon into Junior's mouth hoping to prevent him from swallowing his tongue. Easter was trembling and wide-eyed when Alice appeared at her side. "What in the world is wrong with him?" she asked without a hint of concern.

A wink to Junior told him that his job was done and he reached up and yanked the spoon from his mouth.

"What you trying to do, Easter, kill me?" he cackled as he jumped to his feet and streaked away.

Easter collapsed into a chair and pressed her hand against her clamoring heart. "I'm going to beat that boy black and blue," she breathed.

It took some doing, but the paring knife eventually accomplished the job and the lid popped off and went sailing across the floor. In the safety of her room Alice stared for a long time at the folded piece of yellowed paper before finally taking a deep breath and removing it from the tin. She didn't know what to expect and her heart hammered with anticipation as she carefully undid the folds and smoothed out the creases.

The ink was faded, but not so much that Alice couldn't discern the letters or the word they formed: *HATE.*

CHAPTER 41

After school on Monday, Miss Anthony went to the library to visit, for the umpteenth time, the cherished display. The glass was speckled with tiny fingerprints and she shot an annoyed look at Lollie, who was flipping lazily through a fashion magazine.

"Is it too much to ask to keep the . . ." Miss Anthony declared under her breath as she used the hem of her sweater to wipe away the smudges. While she looped the knitted material across the surface, her eyes lit on the newspaper article with the photograph of a smiling Meredith Tomas shaking the hand of Horace Liveright. Alongside that photo was a shot of the accused Negro plagiarist, E.V. Gibbs.

Her expression lacked emotion, but her eyes were on fire, and it was the fire that Miss Anthony first recognized. What followed that was the echo of Alice's declaration: "My maid reads!"

The realization slammed into Miss Anthony and she doubled over. "Oh. My. God." reverberated through the quiet library like thunder.

Alice skipped down the stairs and was stunned to see Miss Anthony seated on her living room couch, a cup of tea in her hand, nervously bouncing her leg. Shannon sat across from her, holding her chin, something she did when she was listening to something she found extremely interesting or unbelievable. Both women looked up when Alice came down the steps.

Of course Miss Anthony was there to report on Sunday's incident. It was Thursday and Shannon hadn't once brought it up. It was as if it never even happened and now Miss Anthony was there to remind Shannon that it had.

Alice stared at them, waiting for her mother to call her in and begin the interrogation. Shannon stood up and Alice's lips parted, her defense balanced on her tongue. "Hey, Alice," Shannon said. She walked over and pulled the French doors closed.

Alice stood staring at the closed doors and an eerie feeling crept over her. Something was wrong, she thought, as she headed out of the house. Something was very wrong.

Shannon sat back down in her chair and folded her hand over her chin. "Are you sure, Miss Anthony?"

"Yeah, pretty sure."

Shannon leaned back and began moving her hands up and down her bare arms. It was eighty degrees in the house, but suddenly she felt chilled.

"Pretty sure is not enough, you have to be absolutely sure."

Miss Anthony thought about it for a moment, then bobbed her head rapidly up and down. "Yes, I'm sure. I'm absolutely sure."

Shannon sighed. "I—I don't know. If you're wrong I mean it would just start a whole mess of trouble for nothing. You said she did what now?"

"Plagiarized—"

"And that means stealing, right?" Shannon shook her head in disappointment. "Oh gosh, you know how Dobbs is, he'll blow a gasket if he finds out about this. I mean, if you steal a story what won't you steal?" Her eyes wandered over to the Fabergé egg and she wrung her hands. "We have to be sure. Will you drive me down there so that I can see for myself?"

Did they expect Lollie Smith not to ask what was going on? The two of them standing there as still as mannequins staring at the display. Who could ignore that? Had someone scrawled something lewd onto the glass? Was something missing? It would have been easy to steal something from the display. After all, it was just a glass box turned onto its opening. No lock and no key.

Lollie walked over to see what the matter was and when she asked, they told her and said that she shouldn't say anything about it to anyone and Lollie had agreed. But as soon as the two climbed into Miss Anthony's Chevrolet, Lollie Smith was dialing her sister's number.

One call led to another and the telephone circuits in Waycross and the neighboring towns buzzed with the news until finally the phone rang in Odell's Beauty Salon where Easter was just coming out from under the dryer.

Odell herself answered the phone. "Who the hell is E.V. Gibbs? Ain't nobody I ever heard of. She what? The maid o'er at the Eversons'? The Eversons'? Well, who the hell are they?"

Odell listened to the woman jabber excitedly on the other end of the line and after a moment her eyes went wide, then fell on Easter.

"Oh, *those* Eversons."

CHAPTER 42

The way Dobbs heard it, E.V. Gibbs was a murderer. His secretary, Emma Goodkind, had brought him the news, though he had a hard time understanding her—the size of her breasts had a lot to do with it; they filled the room and muffled the sound of her voice. The blouse she wore that day—white with an explosion of red flowers—only compounded the problem.

"Pardon?"

Emma set the stack of papers down on his desk and then folded her arms under her breasts, training them on him like assault missiles.

"I said that maid of yours is causing quite a stir. Seems she killed some white writer woman up in New York way back in the olden days or something."

Dobbs blinked. He'd been able to catch the words *maid*, *killed*, and *olden days*, but not much else. He was about to ask her to repeat herself once more, but Emma was swaying out of the office, her laughter trailing behind her like a scarf. Dobbs picked up the black desk phone and dialed his house and was greeted with the blaring sound of a busy signal.

Easter saw the line of cars out front and her first thought was that someone had died. When she entered through the back door and found a throng of people gathered in the kitchen, a camera bulb flashed and her vision was veiled in a shroud of blue and yellow dots. She'd raised her hand in surprise and when she lowered it again she was back in Harlem, standing outside 409 Edgecombe, clutching her suitcase. The reporters had formed a wall around her and pelted questions at her like stones.

"Is it true you stole Meredith Tomas's story and entered it into the contest as your own?"

"You've been accused of being a thief of literature, what is your response to that accusation?"

"Why did you do it, E.V.?"

Why?

When Easter had posed that very same question to her, Meredith had crinkled her brow and tilted her nose up at her.

"What are you insinuating? It is I who should be asking you that question."

And Easter hadn't had another word to say to her. She went to her bedroom and began to pack.

Rain had scrambled behind her. "I don't understand what's happening! What did you do?" she'd cried, grabbing hold of Easter's arm.

Easter spun around. "What did I do?" The look Easter gave her stopped Rain's heart cold and her hand fell dead away.

And now, in the Eversons' kitchen, Easter bestowed on the spectators that same look before spitting, "What is this, a lynch mob?"

A gasp went up and Shannon's face turned crimson. She caught Easter by the hand and led her through

the crowd, up the stairs, and into the quiet of her bedroom.

CHAPTER 43

The news that E.V. Gibbs, once the literary love child of the Harlem Renaissance, was now nothing but a lowly maid in Waycross, Georgia snaked its way into Tennessee, Kentucky, Ohio, Michigan, and New York. Every day there was a new out-of-state license plate, a new face sitting at the counter of the local diner asking questions and scribbling answers into a notepad. Waycross hadn't seen this much activity since Viola Sanford's cockatiel started reciting the Lord's Prayer. That had been twenty-odd years ago and people still called it a miracle. Well, Dobbs called *this* a miracle too.

He charged a quarter at the door and placed Easter on exhibit, like Ota Benga at the Bronx Zoo, Geronimo at the St. Louis World's Fair, and Saartjie Baartman before all of Europe. Parents set their babies on her lap and snapped photos. She signed autograph books.

Shannon felt like a movie star. The only things missing were floodlights on the lawn and a red carpet.

All of the reporters asked Easter the same question: "Did you plagiarize Meredith Tomas's story?"

And Easter's stock response was always, "God knows the truth and so does Meredith . . . rest her soul."

The last journalist to come to speak to Easter was a tall,

smooth black man with warm eyes and a neat mustache. His name was Roi Ottley and he'd driven all the way down from New York to interview her for the *Amsterdam News*. Roi Ottley had covered World War II, and was the first Negro correspondent for a major newspaper. He'd even had an audience with the Pope!

Roi placed both of his hands over Easter's and looked deep into her eyes like she was someone he had been waiting to meet for a very long time. No one had made her feel that way in ages, and she blushed beneath the weight of it.

He said, "Please call me Roi," when she addressed him as Mr. Ottley.

And she said, "Please call me Easter." But he didn't, he called her Miss Easter.

He had a presence about him and Easter knew immediately that he was an island man because he wore his pride wrapped around his shoulders like a cape.

She asked, "Where were you born?"

"New York City, but my parents are from Grenada."

He spoke in a tone that was just above a whisper, and preferred to sit on the hassock at her feet instead of on the sofa. She felt like a queen.

"You are one of my favorite writers from the Harlem Renaissance," he said, "and I thought *Glorious* was brave and beautiful."

Brave and beautiful? Her little story about a slave girl who escapes to the north and swan dives into the deep end of life? Brave and beautiful . . . Easter beamed with pride.

He asked, "Where have you been all these years?"

Easter leaned back into her chair, folded her hands

in her lap, and thought. She'd been so many places, had seen so many things. She had left Harlem, of course. She couldn't stay there, not after what Meredith had done to her, branding her as a plagiarist, a liar, a thief. She left Harlem and went to Brooklyn, where she briefly secured a job as a maid for a wealthy widow, and then the stock market crashed, forcing her to join the masses of disenfranchised people in a shantytown—a Hooverville in Red Hook. During the day she looked for work, in the evening she stood in soup lines, at night she slept under a box on a bed of newspaper. It was the worst time of her life. Someone stole her shoes right off her feet, she watched a woman die while giving birth. When the soup kitchens ran out of food Easter rummaged for scraps in the garbage. Many a day she dined on her own spit and anger. So destitute was she that pride was an unaffordable luxury; and so she claimed a street corner and begged for change.

She heard about work in Detroit and somehow made her way there and secured a job cleaning toilets at the Ford Motor Company auto plant. On Jefferson Avenue she shared a room with four other women; there were only two beds, so they rotated and every fifth night Easter slept in the tub. When things began to take a turn for the better she bought a ticket to see the Oscar Micheaux film *Murder in Harlem*, and in the velvety darkness of the theater she thought she saw Rain, still stunningly beautiful, smiling out at her from the background, and Easter began to weep.

One year folded into the next, wars were fought and won, fought and lost, people died, babies were born— life churned on and now she was back home in Waycross, Georgia.

Roi pulled a handkerchief from the breast pocket of his suit jacket and held it out to her. Easter stared at the white square of cloth for a long time, not sure why he was giving it to her, and then she licked her lips and tasted her salty tears. She hadn't realized she was crying.

"Oh Jesus, Mary, and Joseph," she sighed as she dabbed at her eyes. "Look what you got me doing. I'm so embarrassed."

"Don't be," Roi said, and waited patiently for her to compose herself before he leaned in and asked, "Are you still writing?"

Easter shifted her eyes away from his piercing stare and shook her head. "No, no," she answered emphatically, "I don't do that anymore."

A still and steady silence fell over them. It was a deep and mournful quiet usually reserved for the dead. It was appropriate.

Roi asked, "Do you know what ever became of Nella or Zora?"

Easter sniffed and shrugged her shoulders. She hadn't known Nella and had only met Zora's acquaintance once or twice. "No, I don't."

Roi looked sad about that. He took Easter's palm in his, raised it to his lips, and planted a chivalrous kiss on the back of her hand. "Miss Easter, it was my immense pleasure to have been in your company. You are an extraordinary woman, and an exceptional writer. I will remember this time with you for the rest of my days."

Easter walked him to the door and watched as he descended the stairs.

When he reached the bottom, he snapped his fingers

and spun around. "My goodness, I almost forgot!" he exclaimed. "Langston sends his regards. He says to tell you that he misses you, that Harlem misses you, and that the world of literature is a better place because of you."

After Roi left, Easter cleared away the plate of cookies, the water glasses ringed with daises, and the napkins they had used to wipe their mouths. She brushed the crumbs from the table into the palm of her hand and dropped them into the pocket of her dress. She returned the hassock to its rightful place, fluffed the pillows on the sofa, lowered the shades in the parlor, and turned on the lamp. She prepared and served dinner, cleared and washed the dishes . . . She did all of this as if in a dream.

When she finally awoke, Alice was standing beside her, holding the tin in her hands. Easter looked down at the girl, down at the tin. "Oh there you are," she breathed, and Alice didn't know if Easter meant her or the ancient object she held.

Alice had used Ivory soap and warm water to clean away the dirt and then polished the metal to a sheen with Vaseline. Easter smiled at the care and effort.

"Did you look inside?"

Alice nodded ashamedly.

"Hmm," Easter sounded as she took it, pried the lid off, removed the tiny bit of paper, and crushed it in her fist. "Hand me them box of matches," she said before tossing the ball of paper into the sink.

They stood—past and future, side by side, hands linked—and watched the flame until there was nothing left but a curl of gray ash.

God balances the sheet in time.
—Zora Neale Hurston

Acknowledgments

The arrival of this book has been six years coming. The story first came to me in 2004 as I sat in my kitchen sipping tea, when suddenly I was aware of the presence of two women, who I will contend until the day I die were the spirits of Zora Neale Hurston and Nella Larsen. I listened to what they had to say and then went into my office and typed out the first twenty pages of what would become this novel.

It was no easy journey. The road from that first day to here was a long, arduous one paved with rejection letters, the death of my father, a near foreclosure, an emotional breakdown, and oceans and oceans of tears.

But we don't do anything in this life alone, and without the love and support of my family, friends, fellow scribes, guides, readers, and God, this book would not have made it into your loving hands.

Author and educator Gloria Wades-Gayle published a book of essays entitled *Rooted Against the Wind*. In it she writes about cultural memory being the "root" and the "polarization of class and race" being the fierce winds.

I write to breath life back into memory to remind African-Americans of our rich and textured history. I also see myself as a "root," and for me the "fierce winds" include the marginalization—the downright segregation—of literature written by people of color.

Whether I am unwilling or unable to conform to the requirements of mainstream publishing is not the question. My only path is to continue to produce works that contribute to the canon of literature created by those writers who came before me. It is, as the young people say, a no-brainer.

Legacies are delicate things. They must be tended to as one would tend an orchid so that it will continue to flourish and provide beautiful blooms. The legacy of African-American literature has been neglected, the works of brilliant writers both published and aspiring—ignored. But I believe that the tides are about to change.

In 1928 Wallace Thurman, the Harlem Renaissance writer and literary radical, said, "The time has come now, when the Negro artist can be his true self and pander to the stupidities of no one, either white or black."

That time has come again.

✳ ✳ ✳

The following books were invaluable to me in writing *Glorious*:

When Harlem Was in Vogue by David Levering Lewis

On Her Own Ground: The Life and Times of Madam C.J. Walker by A'Lelia Bundles

Wrapped in Rainbows: The Life of Zora Neale Hurston by Valerie Boyd

In Search of Nella Larsen: A Biography of the Color Line by George Hutchinson

Negro with a Hat: The Rise and Fall of Marcus Garvey by Colin Grant

As Wonderful as All That? Henry Crowder's Memoir of His Affair with Nancy Cunard 1928–1935 by Henry Crowder and Hugo Speck

Rough Amusements: The True Story of A'Lelia Walker, Patroness of the Harlem Renaissance's Down-Low Culture by Ben Neihart

Look For Me All Around You: Anglophone Caribbean Immigrants in the Harlem Renaissance by Louis J. Parascandola

Ota Benga: The Pygmy in the Zoo by Phillips Verner Bradford and
   Harvey Blume

I would also like to thank the following individuals and
organizations: the MacDowell Colony, which provided me
peace, quiet, and the serenity to become one with the story;
authors Donna Hill, Margaret Johnson Hodge, and Carleen
Brice, who supported me on a multitude of levels and cheered
the loudest when I finally found a home for this novel; the
entire cast of the Harlem Renaissance and especially Zora and
Nella; my publisher Johnny Temple and the staff at Akashic
Books, who took the project on when others wouldn't and
offered me a publishing experience that is inclusive and col-
laborative; my ancestors, spirit guides, and God.

And I thank all of you, the readers who continue to support my work.

I stubbornly remain, rooted against the wind . . .